MIIB
MEN IN BLACK II

THE MOVIE NOVEL

COLUMBIA PICTURES PRESENTS AN AMBLIN ENTERTAINMENT PRODUCTION IN ASSOCIATION WITH MacDONALD/PARKES PRODUCTIONS A BARRY SONNENFELD FILM STARRING TOMMY LEE JONES WILL SMITH 'MEN IN BLACK'™ 2' LARA FLYNN BOYLE JOHNNY KNOXVILLE ROSARIO DAWSON TONY SHALHOUB AND RIP TORN SPECIAL ANIMATION AND VISUAL EFFECTS BY INDUSTRIAL LIGHT & MAGIC MUSIC BY DANNY ELFMAN EXECUTIVE PRODUCER STEVEN SPIELBERG BASED ON THE MALIBU COMIC BY LOWELL CUNNINGHAM STORY BY ROBERT GORDON SCREENPLAY BY ROBERT GORDON AND BARRY FANARO PRODUCED BY WALTER F. PARKES AND LAURIE MacDONALD DIRECTED BY BARRY SONNENFELD

AMBLIN ENTERTAINMENT   COLUMBIA PICTURES

MenInBlack.com

Men in Black II™: The Movie Novel
TM and © 2002 by Columbia Pictures Industries, Inc.
Photography credits:
Melinda Sue Gordon: bottom of page 1, pages 2–4, bottom of page 5, and pages 6–8
Phillip V. Caruso: top of page 5
Industrial Light & Magic: top of page 1
All rights reserved.
Based on the screenplay by Robert Gordon and Barry Fanaro. Story by Robert Gordon.
Printed in the U.S.A.
Library of Congress catalog card number: 2002101107

3 4 5 6 7 8 9 10
❖
First Edition

www.harperchildrens.com

THE MOVIE NOVEL

Written by Michael Teitelbaum
Based on the screenplay by Robert Gordon
and Barry Fanaro
Story by Robert Gordon
Cover photo by Michael O'Neill

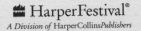

HarperFestival®
A Division of HarperCollinsPublishers

CHAPTER 1

*S*creeeech!

The squealing of tires skidding roughly to a stop shattered the quiet of the deserted downtown street. The front doors of a sleek black sedan flew open. Two men emerged quickly, striding with purpose toward a delicate red flower that stuck up from a steam grate, waiting, as if it had expected their arrival.

Both men were dressed identically in tailored black suits, crisp white shirts, black ties, black shoes, and black sunglasses.

"No fancy stuff, Tee," said the man who had been driving—clearly he was the one in charge. "No heroics. I need you to be cool. We do it by the book this time. Okay?"

"So what you're saying, Jay, is—" Tee replied, but was abruptly cut off.

"Just say 'okay'," Jay said firmly.

"Okay," Tee responded, nodding his head nervously.

"Good," said Jay, walking toward the flower with Tee matching his pace, step for step. "Let's do this, then."

Tee reached the flower first. Looking down, he spoke directly to the red petals, which had closed as tightly as a fist, its slender stalk leaning away from the man who towered over it.

"Hey," Tee called, tapping the stalk with the thick rubber sole of his large black shoe. "Just what exactly do you think you're doing?"

The flower stalk straightened up, rigidly on alert for what might come next.

"Hey, Jeff. How's it going?" Jay asked the flower, his voice calm and friendly. "Why are you here?"

The flower remained perfectly still.

"C'mon, Jeff. You know our arrangement," Jay continued. "You don't travel outside the E, F, and RR subway lines, and in return, you eat all the non-organic garbage you want. Remember? Okay?"

Another moment of silence passed, then Tee squatted down, shouting. "The man's talking to you!"

"Tee," Jay said, trying to calm his partner who was beginning to lose his patience.

Tee grabbed the delicate stem forcefully. "The man

wants to know what you are doing here, worm boy!" he yelled.

The ground trembled as if some enormous force was struggling to break free.

The shaking and rumbling grew louder and more intense, until . . .

Thooom!

With a sound like an exploding bomb, a monstrous worm-shaped creature emerged from beneath the street, shards of asphalt and rock spewing in all directions. The giant worm rose, roaring in rage, its unearthly bellow echoing through the city's concrete canyons.

High above the pavement, Tee desperately grasped the tiny flower stalk that sprouted from the top of the worm-monster's head. The furious creature, known as Jeff, shook its head violently, trying to shake off Tee.

Jay watched Jeff tossing Tee back and forth like a rag doll. "Excuse my partner, Jeff," Jay shouted up to the enormous head high above. "He's new, and . . ."

Jeff reared back, bending his huge body almost in half. Then he lurched his head forward like a catapult and sent Tee flying high into the night sky.

". . . kind of stupid," finished Jay.

Jay watched as his screaming, flailing partner vanished from sight. Jeff slowly lowered his head until the two tiny slits that served as his eyes were even with Jay's face.

"You've gotten big," Jay said casually. "What have you been eating down there?"

Rumble!

Half a block away the sidewalk split in two as Jeff's thick, spiky tail burst through the pavement. All of his long, slinky bulk was now above ground—not exactly the best place for a three-hundred-foot-long, seven-ton worm, Jay thought.

Before Jay could react, Jeff whipped his spike-covered tail around with astonishing speed, slamming into Jay, sending him sailing across the street. Jay crashed into a fruit stand.

Wiping seeds, juice, and rinds from his clothes and face, Jay scrambled to his feet in time to see Jeff slink back down into the hole he had made when he emerged from underground.

"Jeff!" Jay screamed, racing toward the hole. Leaping feetfirst into the huge gash in the street, his right hand pointed back toward the car and he pressed the remote button on his key holder.

Boop-beep.

The car doors locked automatically and the alarm activated just as Jay disappeared into the jagged hole.

CHAPTER 2

Jeff slithered along in the subway tunnel that was only a few feet wider than his body. He felt comfortable again underground, slinking through the complex maze of tunnels that made up the New York City subway system. Back on his home planet, Krydillyon, Jeff and his fellow giant worms would have to dig and burrow for months, even years, to create an underground system as complicated as this one. Since his arrival on Earth, this labyrinth of tunnels served him nicely as a home.

Jay plunged through layers of concrete, rock, and steel, holding his arms close to his chest, keeping his tall thin body as compact as possible, to avoid losing a limb against the jagged sides of the freshly made hole.

Whomp!

Jay landed on Jeff's back near the creature's head and dug in with his heels. He grabbed the fleshy, slimy folds of the giant worm's skin for support. "Way out of line with the tail thing, man!" he shouted as Jeff began to move. "That was uncalled for. Look at my suit!"

Jeff took off as if he had been shot from a cannon, bolting down the dark tunnel with Jay clinging to his back.

"I am citing you for failure to file for movement authorization," Jay recited from memory. "Also, for withholding information from agents of MIB—otherwise known as the Men in Black, appearing as a worm before the populace at large, and—"

Uninterested in any of his violations, Jeff lifted his body abruptly and slammed his head—and Jay's—into the ceiling of the subway tunnel.

"Ow, man!" Jay cried, checking the top of his head for blood. "That's it. Now you've really ticked me off!" He reached into his suit jacket's inside pocket and pulled out a thick metal syringe with a long needle at one end and a thumb-operated plunger on the other. The syringe was filled with worm tranquilizer.

Jamming the syringe into the flower stalk on Jeff's head, Jay pressed the plunger. The air-powered injection shot into Jeff's body. "Sweet dreams, big boy," he said, slipping the syringe back into his pocket. "Just enjoy the pretty colors."

The tranquilizer coursing through Jeff's veins appeared to have the opposite effect from the one Jay had hoped for. The giant worm bolted, racing through the tunnels with Jay hanging on like a bronco rider in a rodeo!

At the Prince Street subway station in fashionable Soho, New Yorkers pride themselves on being unfazed by the unusual, taking the strange in stride. An uptown express train raced through the station with a deafening clatter. People glanced up from their newspapers, books, and handheld video games, then returned to what they were doing. A downtown express train zoomed through the station in the opposite direction. Again a quick group glance.

On the uptown track a giant screeching worm tore through the station, carrying a man in a black suit on its back. People looked up, then back down, then up once more. A little boy from Ohio faced his father with a puzzled expression. His dad just smiled, as he flipped through his New York City guidebook, searching for the section on giant subway worms—a point of interest the travel agent had apparently forgotten to mention.

In the twisting tunnel between stations, Jeff showed no sign of slowing down. Jay continued his speech, with little success. "With the full powers vested in me as an agent of the Men in Black, I hereby place you under arrest. Now pull your big, wiggly self over!"

Jeff ignored him, speeding up and pulling closer to a subway train that raced along the track ahead of him. The giant worm turned his head to the left and snapped it forward, sending Jay flying. The dazed agent landed on top of the last car of the speeding train, sprawled facedown.

Jay raised his head just enough to look around, making sure he kept clear of the tunnel's metal roof supports that now zipped past at a terrifying speed only inches above his head. He saw Jeff coming closer, racing toward the crowded train, his gaping jaws widening, worm drool splattering onto the tunnel walls.

Calling on techniques he perfected during his days as a New York City police officer, Jay crawled along the top of the subway car, inching toward the front.

Jay grabbed two handles on the front of the subway car. He swung his legs down, and landed on the tiny platform just outside the car's service door. He slipped inside and addressed the throng of riders.

"I'm with the Transit Authority, ladies and gentlemen," Jay announced in a serious, booming voice. "Will everyone please move to the first car. We've got a problem. There's a bug in the electrical system."

The passengers ignored him completely.

"PEOPLE!" he shouted. That got their attention. He pointed to the window of the rear door. "*Bug* in the electrical system!" he repeated.

The passengers casually glanced out the back door, then shrieked in terror at the sight of Jeff, his jaws opened wide, about to chomp down on the subway car as if it were a candy bar.

Hysterical passengers raced through the subway car, bolting through the front service door, stepping into the next car.

"Move! Move!" Jay shouted, motioning toward the front of the car with his hands. When the last passenger was out, Jay leaped into the next car, just as Jeff caught up to the train.

Crunch!

Jay looked back and saw Jeff's massive mouth closing around the last subway car. Letting out a satisfied grunt, the giant worm swallowed his appetizer and moved on to the main course.

Jeff devoured the train car by car, as Jay hurried the frantic passengers forward, wondering what he would do when they ran out of cars, if Jeff had not yet run out of appetite.

The service door to the front car slid open with a bang. Thirty screaming people flooded in, the sound of Jeff munching the empty cars behind them filling their minds with horror.

13

The conductor, who operated the train from a small compartment in the front car, stepped from his control panel and held up his hand. "Everyone out before I start knocking heads here!" he shouted to the on-rushing crowd.

Jay shook his head. He reached into his jacket pocket and pulled out his Series Four De-Atomizer gun, the weapon of choice for a top-level agent of the Men in Black.

"Put the hammer down on this thing," Jay ordered.

The conductor straightened his uniform jacket, then stood up as tall as he could. "I am Captain Larry Bridgewater and I decide what happens on this transit transport."

An unearthly bellow filled the subway car. Captain Larry Bridgewater looked out the back window to see Jeff chomping down on the car just behind them.

"Larry just made a decision!" the conductor shouted, ducking back into his control compartment. He slammed the door and threw down the throttle.

Jeff bit down on the back half of the conductor's car, then opened his huge jaws again to finish off his meal. Jay and the cringing passengers stared down the hot, foul-smelling gullet of this humongous eating-machine.

Jay raised his Series Four De-Atomizer and aimed right down Jeff's throat. Jeff ate the gun right out Jay's hand.

Jay balled his hand into a fist and unleashed a powerful uppercut that landed squarely on Jeff's wrinkled chin. The worm's tiny eyes rolled back into his head and the terrifying beast passed out, landing on the track with an earth-shaking thud.

Jay looked down at his still-clenched fist, wondering if the tranquilizer had finally taken effect, but preferring to believe that the former New York Police Department boxing champ still had it when it came to delivering a knockout punch.

CHAPTER 3

The mangled remains of the conductor's car screeched slowly into the 81st Street subway station, half on the tracks and half off. Its twisted metal scraped the edge of the platform and sent sparks flying. The crumpled wreck squealed to a halt.

Inside the car Jay gathered himself, dusted off his suit, and quietly pulled a small cylindrical device from his pocket. His neuralyzer looked like a tiny flashlight with a metal body and a circular light on the tip.

Hysterical passengers wept openly, unable to comprehend what had just happened.

"May I have your attention please," Jay said with authority, slipping on his sunglasses and raising his neuralyzer.

Flash!

An intensely bright light filled the remains of the subway car, bathing everyone in a brilliant white burst. The neuralyzer was doing its job, wiping the astonishing events of the last few minutes from the minds of all those who had witnessed them. In addition, the neuralyzer flash left all who saw it open to suggestion as to what had occurred in the now-missing section of their memory. Jay was ready to fill in those blanks.

"The city of New York thanks you for participating in our drill," he announced in a flat, even tone. "Had this not been a drill, you would have been eaten. We hope you enjoyed our new, smaller, more energy-efficient subway cars. Watch your step as you leave. You *will* have a nice evening."

The doors to the damaged car slid open and the passengers filed out as if this had been just another ride on another typical day. The terrifying chase and attack—so real only seconds earlier—had been completely wiped from their minds and replaced with a story that was as satisfactory as any they might hear during a normal subway ride.

As the crowd left the station, Jay pulled out a communicator. He pressed two buttons on it and spoke softly and quickly. "Men in Black headquarters, this is Agent Jay. We need a clean-up crew at 81st Street and Central Park West. Also, get Transport to tow off what's left of the train."

Immediately dozens of men dressed in black suits, black shoes, and sunglasses identical to Jay's swarmed into the subway station to begin the clean-up process.

"Also," Jay continued, speaking into his communicator. "Revoke Jeff's movement privileges immodiately, and have a Transfer Team take him back to his place at the Chambers Street Station. Oh, and one more thing. Could somebody please check the expiration dates on all the worm tranquilizers!"

Flipping his communicator closed, Jay bounded up the subway stairs. Standing on the top step he blocked people from heading down. "Station's closed, folks," he announced to a line of people waiting to go down into the subway. "Emergency drill, for your safety."

A young man stared at Jay. "Drill?" he said in a shrill voice. "I got a drill for you, pal!" Then turning to his friend, he added, "You believe these jerks?"

"Total losers," the friend replied as the two walked off down Central Park West.

"Yeah, well, you're welcome," Jay called out.

Sighing deeply, Jay strolled over to one of the many benches lining the street bordering Central Park. Behind him in the park, the planetarium at the Rose Center stood majestically, like a great domed spaceship. Inside the planetarium, crowds of visitors watched an amazing show that recreated a night sky dense with stars. It posed the question, is there really life up there?

Looking up into the real night sky, Jay got an immediate answer. He shifted over to the other side of the bench.

Whomp!

Tee landed on the bench, right in the spot where Jay had been sitting, his airborne journey—begun many minutes earlier when Jeff had launched him into the sky—was finally at an end.

"I know, I know," Tee said, straightening his tie. "By the book."

Jay continued staring straight up. "Ever feel like you're all alone in the universe, Tee?" he asked thoughtfully.

"This is a test, right?" Tee replied nervously. "I can get this. Yes . . . No . . . I'm not sure. I'm toast, right?"

Jay stood up and looked back at his partner. "Let me buy you a piece of pie," he offered.

"Really? Thanks, I love pie," said Tee.

The two agents walked slowly up the street. After a brief silence, Tee put his arm around Jay's shoulder and squeezed. "Hey, don't worry, you're not alone in the universe," he said warmly.

"Remove the arm," Jay replied instantly. Tee pulled his arm back down to his side.

After walking several blocks west and a few more

north, they came to a diner. They slid into a booth and ordered coffee and pie. An uncomfortable silence enveloped them as the waitress brought their order.

"Good pie," Tee said after a few bites.

"Yeah," Jay said.

"The place is crowded," Tee added, attempting to keep the conversation going.

"They have good pie," Jay explained.

Tee could not stand it any longer. He put down his fork and wept, quietly at first, then with big heaving sobs. Tears dripped onto the table.

"What are you doing?" Jay asked, looking around, embarrassed. "What is *wrong* with you?"

"You're going to neuralyze me!" Tee cried.

"No, I'm not," Jay replied.

"Yes, you are," Tee insisted. "You brought me to a public place so I wouldn't make a scene."

"You *are* making a scene," Jay pointed out. Then leaning closer, he added, "Let me ask you something. Why did you join the Men in Black?"

"Six years in the Marines," Tee answered immediately. "I like to serve. I like the action. You know, protect the planet and all that."

"In other words, you like being a hero," Jay said.

Tee shrugged and nodded slightly.

"Then you joined the wrong organization," Jay

explained. "You ever heard of James Edwards? Well, he saved eighty-five people on the subway tonight and nobody even knows he exists. And if no one knows he exists, no one can ever love him. Think about that."

Tee nodded and a tear fell onto his pie. "Who cares about love?" he blurted out in a loud, weepy voice. Most of the customers in the diner turned toward them.

"How long have we been partners?" Jay asked impatiently. He silently pulled his neuralyzer from his pocket, keeping it hidden beneath the table.

"We started on February first of this year," Tee replied.

"So that makes it five months and three days," Jay said, fiddling with settings on the neuralyzer beneath the table, while maintaining eye contact with Tee.

"You're thinking that maybe I'm not cut out for this," Tee whined, lowering his head into his hands. "Thinking maybe I'm too weak. Maybe I'm—"

"Too human," Jay finished Tee's sentence.

"Oh, God," Tee cried, sobbing loudly again and blowing his nose into a napkin. "You're getting rid of me! It's over!"

That was it for Jay. This little scene had to end—immediately. He lifted his neuralyzer and pointed the tip toward Tee and—*Flash!*—thousands of hours of work as a Men in Black agent were removed, gone in an instant. Tee stared across at Jay, waiting to be told what to do.

"Get married," Jay suggested, knowing that the neuralyzer had left Tee open to anything he might toss out. "Have a bunch of kids."

"Okay," Tee replied obediently, staring straight ahead. He felt like he was trying to remember something, but couldn't quite put his finger on what it was. With each passing second, though, it became less and less important to remember it at all.

Jay wiped his mouth and stood up. "You were right," he said. "That was good pie." Walking from the table, Jay passed their waitress. "My friend there thinks you're cute," he said pointing to Tee. "He'll take the check."

The waitress smiled and turned to look at Tee, who was still staring straight ahead. When she looked back, Jay was gone.

CHAPTER 4

A golden retriever dashed through a dense thicket of trees, growling and barking. It was followed by a large man who trudged along clutching a leash in his hand and gasping for breath. The bright lights of New York City peeked through the tangle of branches, reminding the man, that despite the country-like surroundings, he was smack in the middle of Central Park at night.

"Harvey!" the man called out between wheezes and coughs. "Heel!"

Harvey looked skyward and spotted something moving through the murky darkness. The dog began to bark even louder.

"You're barking at the moon, Harvey," the man shouted, resuming his awkward trot.

25

The keen-eyed dog looked on as a small space-craft swept across the park, zoomed overhead, then gently landed on a grassy hillside right in front of him.

A hydraulic ramp lowered slowly from the ship with a soft *whoosh*, then a small creature slithered out. It was no more than a thick strand of muscle and nerve—it had no body, no face, no arms or legs. A neural root, to be precise—part brain stem, part nerve-ending, part tendon, all alien.

Harvey barked madly at the strange creature who rose up like a cobra, but was in fact tiny compared to the full-grown dog. The spaceship itself was only two feet across; the alien was only a few inches long, like an oversized earthworm.

The neural-root creature let loose a sound that was half shriek and half roar, painful to Harvey's sensitive ears and terrifying beyond anything the dog had ever experienced.

Harvey whimpered, then turned and ran off, fol-lowed closely by his winded master who never even bothered to look down.

The neural creature crawled along the ground like a snake searching for prey. It came upon a magazine open to an ad for ladies' lingerie. The image of a beautiful ravened-haired model posing in black lin-gerie practically leaped off the page. The creature stared at the photo for a moment then shook violently.

The tiny stalk grew in all directions at once, sprouting

arms, legs, and hair. The shape of a woman's torso began to evolve from the once single strand of living tissue. Within seconds, the alien had transformed into the exact likeness of the model in the ad. Having snatched up the magazine with her now-human hand, the alien stared at the page, then looked down at her newly formed body.

Suddenly she felt a knife pressed against her throat. Its razor-sharp blade glistened in the moonlight. "Hey, pretty lady," said a deep voice from behind.

The alien glanced over her shoulder and saw a man in a leather coat clutching the knife which now pushed harder against her windpipe. He grabbed her arm and pulled her to an isolated grove of trees.

"Stay calm, don't make any noise," the man ordered gruffly. Then he licked the alien's all-too-human-looking neck. "Umm, you taste good."

With a swiftness beyond comprehension, the alien reached over her shoulder, grabbed her attacker, and pulled him forward over her head. Shoving the man into her mouth—which had now transformed into a huge, gaping cavern—she swallowed him whole.

"Umm," she cooed. "You taste good, too."

Several blocks away, a dark-haired man wearing a backpack paced nervously around a small, dumpy apartment. The place was filled with piles of clutter—newspapers, magazines, video games, CD and DVD players, video recorders—the toys and debris of modern pop culture.

"Shut up, Charlie!" the man screamed, though there was no one else in the apartment. He looked over his shoulder at the backpack and continued. "I'm tired of you constantly talking behind my back!"

He opened the refrigerator and stared at the barren shelves. "Only one beer," he muttered.

"What about me?" cried a muffled voice from the backpack.

"Shut up!" the man yelled. "I'll share."

"Forget it," replied the voice. "I know where your mouth has been."

Slamming the refrigerator door shut, the man was startled to find himself face to face with what looked like a beautiful model.

"Hey!" the man shouted, dropping his beer bottle to the floor. It shattered, sending glass and beer spreading across the kitchen. "Who are you? How'd you get in here?"

A head popped out of his backpack and extended up on a long neck, peering over the man's shoulder at the gorgeous woman before him. "Hey, Scrad," said the head, which was actually attached to the man's shoulders. "Who's your friend?"

The woman raised her hands, and long, sinewy neural roots extended from her fingertips revealing her true unearthly form. One powerful root wrapped around Scrad's neck, the other grabbed Charlie's neck that protruded from the backpack. The roots slowly tightened.

"Serleena, it's you!" gasped Scrad, coughing and choking. "W—Why didn't you just say so?"

Serleena released Scrad and Charlie, withdrawing her deadly tentacles back into her fingertips. The two-headed alien dropped to the floor, both heads struggling for breath.

Looking once again fully like the model she had morphed into, Serleena glanced around the apartment, then shook her head disdainfully. "Look at this junk!" she shrieked. "High-definition TV, high-speed Internet connection, *People* magazine.

"I hired you for a mission," Serleena said. "And you went Earthling on me! You went native, buying into all this nonsense!"

Scrad replied quickly. "We hate Earth."

Charlie lifted his head, extending his extremely long neck to its full height. His head was now higher than Scrad's. "We were just trying to fit in."

Ignoring them, Serleena continued. "Do you have the information?" she asked.

"Information?" Scrad repeated nervously.

"I sent you an interstellar fax," Serleena growled. "Didn't you get it?"

"Oh, a fax," Charlie said, trying to sound casual. "Well, you see, our toner cartridge went bad. *You* try finding a replacement for a Kylothian Z-11 fax machine here on Ear—"

Serleena leaped at Scrad and Charlie. "Yes or no?" she shouted. Neural roots shot from her fingers again, this time entering their ears.

"Ahhh!" Scrad and Charlie bellowed in agony, Serleena's muscular tentacles burrowing directly into their brains.

"We couldn't find the Light!" Scrad managed to get out through the torturous throbbing in his head. "But we tracked it to a guy who might know where it is. He runs a pizza place on Spring Street."

Instantly the neural roots retracted into Serleena's fingers. "Take me there," she said flatly, turning and striding out of the apartment.

Scrad and Charlie struggled to find their balance, dizzy from the excruciating pain.

"Let's go before she does something else to us," Scrad said as he grabbed onto a chair to steady himself.

"But we're going to miss *Friends*," whined Charlie. "You know it's my favorite show!"

"Shut up," said Scrad. On his way to the door, he stopped for a second at their audio-video cabinet and pressed a button on a sleek black machine.

"Video recorder," said Charlie, smiling. "Beauty, Scrad. I love this planet." Then they hurried after Serleena and slammed the apartment door behind them.

CHAPTER 5

Spring Street in the heart of Soho was a busy place by day. But at night it flowed with even more life and noise, the explosive energy of a city that never stopped moving.

Tourists moved excitedly in and out of art galleries and antiques shops breathing in culture, both contemporary and ancient. Young musicians hurried along the sidewalk to gigs or rehearsals, instrument cases slung over their shoulders.

Sooner or later everyone got hungry. For many on Spring Street, that meant popping into Famous Ben's Pizza for a slice. The small neighborhood pizzeria had been part of downtown life for over twenty years.

Inside the restaurant, Ben handed a plaque to a young woman who worked for him. Ben was a hard-working man in his fifties. He had a kind face that spoke of someone satisfied with his job, his life, and his position as a beloved fixture in a classic New York neighborhood.

The young woman who happily accepted the plaque had worked for Ben since she was old enough to have a job. Her pretty face beamed with a bright smile as she looked at the picture of herself on the highly polished piece of dark wood. Beneath the photo the words, BEN'S PIZZA EMPLOYE OF THE MONTH . . . LAURA VASQUEZ were engraved onto a small brass rectangle. Her eyes peered out of the photo from beneath her glossy brown hair.

"Ben," said Laura, squeezing his hand. "I don't know what to say."

"People will look at that plaque for years to come," Ben announced proudly, "and you know what they'll say?"

"That 'employee' is spelled wrong?" Laura replied.

"Hey, they charge by the letter," Ben explained, shrugging. "No. What people will say is, 'imagine that, a big shot like her used to work here'."

"Ben," Laura said, "thanks."

"Hey, you deserve it," Ben said emphatically, then quickly added, "Bring up a couple of cases of soda from the basement, would ya?"

"Ah," Laura replied. "Fame is fleeting. I'll be right back."

Laura turned and hurried into the restaurant's back room. She bounded down the stairs to the basement and loaded several cases of soda onto a small service elevator, hit the Up button, then bounded back up the stairs to meet the cases.

As the elevator doors slid open, she heard a commotion coming from the front of the store. Laura opened the door between the back room and the main dining area just a crack and peeked out to see a beautiful, oddly dressed woman and a man wearing a backpack standing next to Ben. They hovered over him menacingly.

"Where is it . . . Ben?" the woman asked. "That is what you're calling yourself on this planet, isn't it?"

"I don't know what you're talking about," Ben replied.

Laura gasped in horror when she saw two tentacles extend from the woman's fingers and grab Ben by the throat. She quietly closed the door, picked up the phone, and dialed 911. "I'd like to report a robbery at—"

Bam!

The back door to the pizzeria blew open and the wind slammed it into the wall. Laura stared out the door, looking at the store's back alley. Then she heard footsteps rushing from the main dining area. She hung up the phone and frantically searched for a place to hide.

Laura ducked under a table near some supplies, but peeked out just enough to see the man with the backpack hurry into the room. As he closed the back door, Laura heard the woman call out from the front.

"Do you idiots see anything back there?" screeched the powerful voice.

Idiots? thought Laura. *I only see one guy.*

"The wind just blew the door open, that's all," the man yelled back.

Then a head popped out of his backpack, rising up next to the head that had just spoken. "Nothing out of the ordinary!" the second head added.

Laura's eyes opened wide in amazement. Was this some sort of ventriloquist act? A puppet show? The head in the backpack looked so real! When the man had returned to the front of the pizzeria, Laura slipped quietly from the cabinet and resumed her place at the door, watching the strangers interrogate Ben.

"For twenty-five years I've traveled the universe looking for it," the woman revealed. "But it never left Earth, did it 'Ben.' You kept it here."

"Look, I don't know what you are talking about, lady," Ben said gruffly. "But I've got a pizza place to run."

"And I'm running out of time," the woman replied angrily. "Where is the Light of Zartha?"

"I swear I don't know what you're—"

Ben was cut short as the woman removed her tentacles from his throat and placed a single finger onto his forehead. "While you've hidden here like a coward, we've been preparing to invade your planet," she explained. "Once I have the Light, Zartha will be ours!"

Ben's face hardened. There was no point in playing his little game any longer. "You're too late, Serleena," he said. "Tomorrow the Light will leave the Third Planet and soon it will be back home. Then you'll wish you never started any of this!"

"I didn't come all this way to leave empty-handed," Serleena snarled. Then she dug a fingernail into Ben's forehead and yanked down hard, tearing his skin open. She ripped it in half like an old paper bag.

Ben's human skin dropped in a heap onto the floor, revealing his true alien form—that of a glowing starfish, hovering in midair.

"Sorry you made the trip for nothing, Serleena," said the alien who moments before had been Ben. A low hum came from the starfish creature, then it exploded into a thousand luminescent pieces. They twinkled in the air like a starry sky, then vanished into nothingness.

"I can't believe we got nothing out of him," Charlie cried, popping up from the backpack. "We don't even know if it's on Earth or not!"

"He said it was leaving the Third Planet!" Serleena raged on. "It's here, you idiot!"

"Third Planet," Scrad leaned back and whispered. "As in *Third Rock from the Sun*."

"Oh," Charlie whispered back. "I never got that until now."

Serleena ignored them. "Now I know it's on Earth," she said through clenched teeth. "And I also know who can tell me where it is." Then she stormed from the pizzeria, followed closely by Scrad and Charlie.

In the back room, Laura sat on the floor. She trembled uncontrollably and cried softly, her tears dripping onto the dank floor. She had just seen Ben—her boss, her friend, a man she had known for as long as she could remember—have his skin torn from his body like a cheap suit, turn into a starfish, then explode. Her mind reeled and her head throbbed.

CHAPTER 6

The stately, stone building which served as head-quarters for the Men in Black rose high into the Manhattan skyline. Looking at this impressive structure, passersby might have thought they were looking at the headquarters of a bank, an insurance company, or a Wall Street brokerage house.

There were no visible clues to the fact that deep within this dignified edifice, creatures from thousands of galaxies worked side by side with the agents of the Men in Black to maintain peace and to keep the knowledge that humans were not alone in that universe a secret.

Jay strode through the massive front door into the main lobby of Men in Black headquarters, his footsteps echoed off the high ceiling and marble walls.

"Don't you ever go home?" asked the security guard from behind his folded newspaper. The guard had worked there for many years, but could recall few agents who put in the hours that Jay did.

"What are you, the hall monitor?" Jay shot back.

"You know, you wouldn't be so cranky if you got a full eight hours sleep every once in a while," the guard replied.

Jay stepped into the elevator at the far end of the lobby.

When the doors reopened he walked briskly into the main hall. The place was a beehive of activity. Everywhere Men in Black agents and aliens—with wings, tails, multiple eyes, legs, arms, and heads—worked busily at computer terminals or laboratory stations. Some took notice of Jay's entrance, but most simply went about their business—just another day at the office.

Jay walked past two agents, Bee and Dee, who were having a discussion. They were face to face, only Dee stood on the ground and Bee stood on the ceiling, hanging upside-down, his suction shoes gripping the ceiling tiles.

As Jay passed a large insect-like alien with eight legs, pincers, and a shiny black shell, he called out to an agent. "Double-check his visa," Jay ordered, pointing to the alien. "Sephalopods have been making

40

counterfeits at the Kinko's on Canal Street."

Two agents pushed a dead three-headed alien across the hall's main floor on a gurney. "Whose bright idea was it to bring a dead Tricrainasloph through Passport Control?" Jay asked, shaking his head in disappointment. "We're slipping, people."

Jay turned and spotted several agents rolling a small prison cell across the floor. The bars of this cell were actually powerful beams of light, stronger than the strongest metal bars ever used in a conventional prison.

Sitting quietly within the cell, an elderly human-looking man looked up at Jay and scowled.

"Jarra," Jay said to the man. "Long time."

"Five years and forty-two days in this cage, thanks to you," Jarra snarled. "You count every one when you're locked away like a primate."

"You shouldn't have been siphoning off our ozone to sell on the black market," Jay explained with a shrug. Then turning to one of the agents pushing the cage he asked, "What's Jarra doing here?"

"We're moving him to supermax security," the agent replied. "He hasn't been playing well with his fellow in-mates. He killed two Plasma Beetles from Andromeda."

"'Killed' is such an ugly word." Jarra sneered as his prison cage was rolled away.

At the far side of the main hall Jay reached an unmarked door. He knocked twice, pulled the door

41

open, and stepped into a large office. Jay walked past a huge window that looked out onto the main floor, then pulled up a chair opposite a large wooden desk.

"Good work in the subway," said the man behind the desk. "I remember Jeff when he was no bigger than a gummy worm."

"Sewage does a body good, Zed," replied Jay. "What else have you got for me?"

Zed took a deep breath and leaned back in his chair. As leader of the Men in Black, the short, muscular man had seen many agents come and go, but few had the nonstop desire to work that Jay displayed every single day.

"Look out that window, Jay," Zed said softly, nodding his head toward the activity on the other side of the glass. "See all the guys in black suits? They work here too. We've got it covered."

"Zed—" Jay protested, but Zed cut him off.

"Listen friend," the supervisor lectured. "Dedication's one thing, but if you let it, this job will eat you up and spit you out whole. You want to look like me when you hit fifty . . . ish?"

Jay stood up and walked to the door. "If you need me, I'll be in the gym," he said, pulling the door open.

"We had a killing earlier," Zed admitted. "Ben's Pizza, Spring Street. Take Tee with you and file a report."

"Uh, Tee. Yeah," Jay said nervously. "I guess you heard about what happened."

At that moment, a small dog trotted into the office carrying a folder in his mouth. He dropped the folder onto a chair then looked up at Zed. "Some passports that need your signature. No rush." Then turning to Jay he added. "Hey, Jay. How's it going?"

"Thanks, Frank," Zed said to the dog. In truth this was no dog, but an alien who had chosen the form of a small pug—flat nose, wrinkled skin, short stubby legs, tough New York attitude—during his stay on Earth.

"Sure thing, boss," Frank replied.

Zed looked back at Jay. "You are not authorized to neuralyze Men in Black personnel under any circumstances!"

"Zed, the man was crying in a diner," Jay pleaded.

"I hate that," Frank chimed in.

"I don't need a partner," Jay said angrily, looking down at Frank.

"You need a partner," Zed corrected him.

"I'll be his partner," Frank volunteered, looking up at Zed hopefully.

Zed looked from Jay to Frank, then back to Jay. Then he nodded and pointed to the door.

A few minutes later Jay and Frank walked quickly through the Men in Black vehicle compound. Jay was in his black suit, white shirt, and black tie, and Frank in a dog-sized black suit, white shirt, and black tie. When they reached Jay's car, he pressed a button on his key chain. The black sedan chirped twice. Then the engine turned over, the car rolled forward, and the two front doors popped open.

"I really appreciate the shot, Jay," Frank said, hopping up into the passenger seat. "I never thought I was going to make it out of the mailroom."

Jay looked across the car at his new partner. "You're supposed to be a dog, remember?" Jay explained. "Lose the suit."

Jay hit the gas and sped from the garage, tires squealing. Frank, playing the role of a dog, stuck his head out the window, tongue wagging, slobber flying. A glob blew back into the car and landed on Jay's jacket.

"Oh, real nice," Jay moaned, looking down at the dog spit making its way down his lapel. "Get your head in the car!"

"Sure thing, partner," Frank replied, dropping down onto the seat, thrilled to be a real agent at last.

When they reached Ben's Pizza, Jay and Frank found Men in Black agents dusting for fingerprints and scanning the restaurant with various alien detection devices.

"What do we got?" Frank asked one of the agents in a take-charge tone of voice.

Jay looked down at him, cocked one eyebrow, then asked the same agent, "What do we got?"

"There's a phosphorus residue on the wall and floor," the agent explained, pointing to the area where Ben had exploded. "We've sent the samples back for analysis."

"Hey, Jay!" Frank called out from across the room. "Look at this."

Jay joined his new partner next to the empty sack of fake skin that had covered Ben's body.

"Zero-percent body fat!" Frank quipped.

Jay ignored him. "Where's the witness?" he asked the first agent.

"She's back there," replied the agent, pointing to an open door. "She saw everything and is actually taking it pretty well." Then he handed Jay a napkin.

Jay looked down at the napkin and saw the pizza parlor's logo—a triangular slice of pizza resting on its side. The top corner of the slice pointed up to an image of the Statue of Liberty in the distance. Above the statue a single star twinkled in a night sky. Jay flipped the napkin over and saw the name "Vasquez" scrawled sloppily on the crinkled white surface.

Slipping the napkin into his pocket, Jay peered into the back room and saw Agent Cee interrogating a pretty, young woman.

"No, you listen to me!" Laura Vasquez shouted at Cee. "I don't answer any more of your questions until you answer mine. I want someone to tell me what happened here!"

"I'd better handle this," Jay said walking toward the back room. He turned to Frank. "Alone. The whole talking dog thing might not be good for her right now."

"What do you want me to do?" Frank asked.

"Sniff around," Jay replied.

"Funny, partner," Frank groaned. "Real funny."

CHAPTER 7

When Jay stepped into the pizzeria's back room, he found Agent Cee trying unsuccessfully to calm Laura down.

"Take a deep breath, ma'am," Agent Cee said. "Everything's all right."

"No, everything is *not* all right," Laura said. "Number one, who were those creatures who killed Ben? Number two, what did Ben turn into?"

"And number three," Jay added stepping up beside Laura. "What part of this is she supposed to feel all right about?"

"Yeah," Laura said defiantly. "What *he* said."

"I'm Agent Jay," he said to Laura, motioning for Agent Cee to leave. "And you are?"

"Not crazy," Laura said forcefully. "Your pals are pretending that they don't believe me, but I know they know I know what I saw."

"Why don't you just tell me what you saw," Jay said calmly. "Mrs. . . . ?"

"Miss," Laura corrected Jay. "Vasquez. Laura Vasquez. If I answer your questions, will you answer mine?"

Jay nodded and Laura continued.

"Okay," she spoke slowly. "I saw a two-headed guy. I saw a woman in leather with tentacles coming out of her hands. I saw her . . ." Laura paused, noticing Jay staring right into her eyes. "You think I'm crazy, don't you! Fine. So I didn't see her—"

"Rip the skin off his body," Jay finished without any change in the calm expression in his voice.

"Rip the skin off his body," Laura repeated, looking at Jay suspiciously.

"Actually it's not skin," Jay explained. "It's a proto-plasma polymer, similar in makeup to the bubble gum you find in baseball cards."

"This is something you run into a lot?" she asked.

"Never south of Twenty-Third Street," Jay replied without the slightest trace of humor in his voice.

"Who are you?" Laura asked. "Really."

"Hey, what was the last thing you ate prior to the incident?" Jay asked, changing the subject.

"Calzone," Laura replied.

"Spinach?" he asked.

"No, mushroom," answered Laura, a little confused.

"You need pie," said Jay as he grabbed Laura's hand and led her out of the pizzeria.

Laura followed Jay out to his car. A short while later she found herself in a diner, eating pie and drinking coffee. "They kept asking Ben about a light," she told Jay, finally believing that he didn't think she was crazy. "A Light of Zartha, or something like that."

Laura sighed deeply. Here she was discussing this crazy situation with a total stranger, as if it was something that happened every day. Her hand started to shake.

"Are you okay?" Jay asked.

"An hour ago a man I've known my whole life vanished right in front of my eyes," she explained, trying to stay calm. "He was killed by a woman who had things coming out of her fingers, and her accomplice was a two-headed guy. What I saw couldn't possibly exist, yet I know in my heart that I saw it. Tell me what I'm supposed to believe."

Jay stared into Laura's eyes debating what to say next. His professional training told him to make up a story, but he knew that he couldn't. "I'm a member of a secret organization that polices and monitors alien activity on Earth," he blurted out. "Ben was an alien and so were the people who killed him. I don't know why they did it, but I promise you I'm going to find out. Okay?"

"Okay," Laura replied calmly, her eyes locked onto Jay's.

He slowly reached into his pocket and pulled out his neuralyzer. "Listen, Laura. I'm sorry," he said, adjusting the settings on the tiny device. "But now that I've told you all that I'm going to have to—"

"Kill me, right?" Laura said.

"No," Jay explained, holding up the neuralyzer. "This will just help you to forget what you saw. One little flash and everything in your mind will be back the way it was."

"After you flash me," Laura began. "If I see you again, will I remember you?"

"No," Jay replied. "But I'll see you, even if you don't see me."

"That must be lonely," Laura said smiling sadly at Jay. "Keeping secrets, never really knowing anyone."

Before he could say a word, Jay's communicator beeped. "Excuse me," he said, getting up from the table and walking to a corner of the diner.

"Zed, what's up?" he said softly into the small cell-phone-like device.

"I need your report," Zed's voice chirped from the communicator's tiny speaker. "Talk to me."

"The pizza guy was a Zarthan," Jay explained,

speaking quietly, cupping his hands around the communicator. "The killer wasn't. Any unauthorized ship landings?"

"One," Zed reported. "Central Park, West Seventy-Second Street off the Drive. About four hours ago. It fits."

"On my way," Jay said, flipping the communicator shut and walking quickly back to the table where Laura sat. She waited patiently to have her memory erased.

"I have to go," he said, heading for the door.

"What about the flashy thing?" Laura asked.

Jay slipped the neuralyzer into his pocket. "I'll flash you some other time," he said, disappearing out the diner's front door.

When Jay reached the car, Frank was waiting in the passenger's seat. "Did you tell her you loved her?" Frank asked as Jay slipped in behind the wheel.

"She's a witness to a crime," Jay said flatly, starting up the engine. "That's it."

"Yeah, sure, yada, yada," Frank said in a sing-song voice. "I didn't see any neuralyzer flash coming from that diner. You're attracted to her. She's not even my species and *I'm* attracted to her!"

Jay pressed down hard on the gas and peeled away from the curb, slamming Frank back into his seat. Tearing through the city at top speed, the two agents soon arrived at Central Park West and Seventy-Second Street. They pulled up to the curb, flung their doors open, and rushed from the car.

As soon as they entered the park they spotted Men in Black trucks parked everywhere and agents swarming around the area taking soil samples and searching trees and benches for clues.

"Coming through," Frank announced loudly, pushing his way into the crowd. "Men in Black brass. Look sharp!"

"Frank!" Jay snapped at his partner. "Shhh!"

In the center of the mass of activity a small, yellow plastic tent had been erected. An agent posted at the entrance nodded at Jay and Frank as they entered.

Inside, several agents stood in front of a tiny spacecraft that measured less than two feet across. It sat on the ground in exactly the spot where it had landed. Jay picked up a long tubular probe, then signaled for the other agents to leave the tent.

Jay pulled out his communicator and plugged one end of the probe into it, then inserted the other end of the probe—which contained a light and a tiny video camera—into a small opening in the spacecraft.

"Zed, you're all patched in," he announced into the communicator. "You should be able to see everything I see up on the monitor at headquarters."

"The picture's coming through fine on this end, Jay," Zed reported. "Talk to me."

Jay peered into an eyepiece as he snaked the probe around the tiny ship. Both Jay and Zed saw the interior of what was obviously the high-tech, heavily armed vessel of a warrior. Spare, sleek, and packed with weapons.

"Looks like a Kylothian Class C battle cruiser," Jay reported. "This baby's loaded with antimatter torpedoes."

"Well, happy birthday to me," Zed muttered, gritting his teeth and running his fingers through his hair.

"The witness at the pizza place said the aliens who did in her boss were looking for some kind of light," Jay said, continuing to move the probe around inside the ship. "Light of . . . something or other."

"Zartha," Zed replied. "The Light of Zartha."

"Right," Jay said. "What is it?"

"Something that was settled a long time ago," Zed said mysteriously.

"Zed, talk to me," Jay insisted.

"Twenty-five years ago, the Zarthans came to Earth asking us to hide the Light of Zartha from their enemies, the Kylothians," Zed explained. "The Light is a power source, like the sun—more powerful, in fact. Just different physics. In any case, in the wrong hands, it's a big bad mojo."

"We couldn't let them hide it here," Jay said, starting to put the pieces together.

"Exactly," Zed replied. "The Zarthans are a nice

bunch, but I ordered the Light off the planet. The Kylothians would have blown up the Earth."

"So if it's gone," Jay wondered. "Why would the Kylothians be back here looking for it?"

"No logical explanation." Zed sighed.

"Are you sure it's not still here?" Jay asked, removing the probe and disconnecting it from the communicator. He had seen all he needed to see of this ship.

"I gave the order myself," Zed explained. "My best agent carried it out. It's as if I gave the order to you."

"Then why don't you just ask the agent?" Jay suggested.

"Can't," was all Zed replied.

"He's dead?" Jay asked.

"Sort of," Zed said. "He lives in Massachusetts."

Jay stopped dead in his tracks. "Oh, no," he muttered. "No, it can't be. Not Kay!"

"I'm afraid so," said Zed. "Earth's very existence may rest on what Kay knows. Too bad you wiped out his entire memory of it. So, here are my orders to you. Bring him in.

"Now!"

CHAPTER 8

The tiny town of Truro, Massachusetts, looked like thousands of other small towns around the United States.

The Truro post office was a red brick building with tall white columns in front—the only official government building in town. People strolled in and out carrying packages, picking up mail from their P.O. boxes, or just stopping on the long front steps to chat with neighbors.

Heads turned and people whispered and pointed, as the sleek black sedan pulled up to the curb in front of the post office. The driver's side door flew open with an urgency rarely seen in this sleepy town. Jay sprang from the car, turning back and leaning his head into the window.

"Stay!" he ordered, pointing a finger at Frank who sat, panting, in the passenger's seat.

"You know, I may look like a dog," Frank growled. "But actually, I only play one here on Earth."

Jay ignored his partner and entered the building. The inside of the post office appeared to be even more frozen in time than the outside. Plaster walls painted a sickly institutional green ran up to a drop ceiling of white plaster panels and long florescent lights, many of which blinked on and off.

Jay walked among the customers, sizing up the place, looking at the various counters, stamp machines, and service windows. The main counter contained several windows. Seated behind the center window, holding court, was Jay's former partner, Kay.

Kay had recruited Jay, back when he was a New York City cop, brought him in to the Men in Black, and trained him. In crucial situations Jay still heard Kay's voice in his head repeating some small piece of advice that helped turn a deadly situation into a victory for the covert agency, and in turn, for planet Earth.

Jay recalled the day he neuralyzed Kay, wiping out all his memories of the Men in Black. Kay had finally had enough of the secret-agent life and craved some kind of normal existence. He sure got that, Jay thought. He felt a bit sad, seeing a former top agent selling stamps and weighing packages. But to Kay, he was simply doing his job.

"Good people of Truro, may I have your attention," Kay began as if he was lecturing a group of rookie agents. "In order for us to expedite your shipping needs, I'd like to remind you that all packages must be properly wrapped. Brown paper and double twist twine are the preferred media. Thank you for your time."

Jay stepped up to the window. "Kay?" he asked tentatively.

"C," Kay replied pointing to the letter above his window. "Express mail, two-day air."

"Kevin," Jay said, reading Kay's name tag. It was the first time Jay had ever heard Kay's real name. "You don't remember me, but we used to work together."

Kay looked Jay over from head to toe, staring for a few seconds at his suit. "I never worked at a funeral home," he said flatly. "Something I can do for you, slick?"

Jay took a deep breath. "Okay, straight to the point," he began. "You are a former agent of a top secret organization that monitors the activities of extra-terrestrials on Earth. We are the Men in Black. We have a situation. We need your help."

"There's a free mental-health clinic on the corner of

Lilac and East Valley," Kay replied, unfazed by Jay's startling statement. "Next!"

"Look, you were told that your memory loss was due to a coma," Jay insisted. "But there wasn't any coma, okay? It was a cover! You have to admit that there are sections of your life that are missing from your memory."

"Who are you?" Kay asked, squinting, searching Jay's face for a flicker of recognition. None came.

"The more important question," Jay began, leaning in close to Kay's face, "is who are *you*?"

"Postmaster of Truro, Massachusetts," Kay stated in an official tone. "And I am ordering you to leave the premises." Then he stood and shouted, "Break!"

Kay left his position behind the window and headed for the mail-sorting area, with Jay close on his heels. As Kay entered the area, a young post office employee dropped a full pot of steaming coffee that shattered and spread across the floor.

"We have a breach!" Kay announced. "Farrell, cordon off the area. Billings, full perimeter wipe-down. Let's move, people!"

"Listen to yourself!" Jay shouted. "Who talks like that?" Pulling a palm-sized device from his pocket, Jay scanned the various employees, some rushing to clean up the coffee spill, others slowly going about their jobs.

Jay's alien detection unit revealed that the postal

workers were, in fact, a wide variety of aliens. "*Hytuu saee habbilmuu*," Jay blurted out in a loud, clear voice.

At the sound of an alien tongue being spoken, the various races of creatures relaxed their disguises. Kay looked on in amazement as the alien employees revealed their beaks, wings, tentacles, tails, and extra heads.

Jay pulled open the door of a mail-sorting machine, revealing a twelve-armed alien using all of its limbs to sort letters at an eye-blurring rate.

"Why do you think you ended up working at a post office?" Jay asked Kay, as the aliens reestablished their human identities. "They're all aliens here. That's why you feel so comfortable."

Kay stared at Jay for a moment, then turned and stormed from the post office with Jay following close behind.

"You look up at the night sky and feel like you understand more about what's going on up there than you do down here!" Jay shouted, matching Kay's pace step for step. "You get a feeling in your gut like you don't know who you are, and it eats at you every day of your life."

Out on Main Street, Kay continued walking toward a post office truck, ignoring Jay's words. Jay stopped at the door to his sedan. "If you want to know who you really are, come take a ride with me!" Jay shouted at Kay's back. "If not, well, people are waiting for their

TV Guides. It's up to you." Then Jay whipped open the door and slipped in behind the wheel.

Jay started up the car and Frank scrambled to the backseat. Just as Jay was about to pull away, the front passenger door swung open and Kay slid in.

"Just going for a ride," Kay said nervously. "Things don't add up. Hear what I'm saying, junior?"

"Hey, Kay!" Frank called out from the backseat. "Long time, no see."

Kay turned around and found himself face to face with a talking dog.

"That's your replacement, Kay," Jay stated as he pulled away from the curb. "So watch who you're calling 'junior'." Turning off of Main Street and heading toward the interstate highway, Jay picked up speed, rushing from this tiny town as fast as the car would take him.

CHAPTER 9

Jay, Kay, and Frank walked briskly through the lobby of Men in Black headquarters.

"Good to see you again, Kay," the guard said, not even glancing up from his paper.

"Good to see you, too," Kay replied. "Whoever you are."

They headed to the elevator at the far end of the lobby. The three stepped in and the door slid shut.

Jay led the way out into the main hall of Men in Black operations. A low buzz spread throughout the huge room as agents and aliens alike recognized the man who had been one of their top operatives.

"Welcome back," one agent said.

"Agent Kay," another added, nodding respectfully.

A very excited agent spotted Kay from across the

61

room. He rushed over and eased Jay out of the way with his hip. Then he extended his hand. "You're Agent Kay!"

"So they tell me," Kay said, shaking the agent's hand.

"This is really an honor," he said. "Gee. I'm Agent Gee. You, sir, are a legend. The most respected agent in Men in Black history. The most feared human in the universe."

"Excuse me, Gee," Jay interrupted. "But if you don't mind, we've got a planet to save!"

Jay hustled Kay toward Zed's office. On the way they passed a group of agents performing an autopsy on a dead alien. The blue-and-green creature had four arms and six legs. "Hey, Kay!" shouted one of the agents, elbow deep in alien guts. "You're back."

"Yup," said Kay. He was still extraordinarily con-fused and had no memory whatsoever about any part of his life as an agent, but seeing the reaction he created just by walking through this room made Kay believe that maybe the wild story Jay had told him could actually be true.

"Any idea what might have done this guy in?" the agent asked, lifting his arms from the alien's open body cavity. Blue slime, green blood, and something resembling a spleen dripped back down into the opening.

"I had a cousin about that size," Kay volunteered. "Choked on a Lifesaver."

"Choking," said the agent, as Kay walked away. "That's a possibility. Boy, it's good to have him back."

"Yeah," replied Jay, starting to get a bit fed up with all the fuss. "I'm throwing a party for him later."

Jay, Kay, and Frank entered Zed's office. The three agents stood before their boss's desk.

"Kay!" exclaimed Zed, grasping his hand and patting him on the back. "I'm afraid Earth might be in a bad way, and you, my friend, may be the one man who can save it."

"Well, you know our motto," Kay replied. "Neither rain nor snow."

"Good man," Zed said, pointing to the door. "Get him armed and up to speed, then take him over to Deneuralyzation. We need that memory back, Jay. And fast!"

Jay and Kay rushed from the office, with Frank close behind.

"Uh, Frank," Zed called out, causing the pug to stop and turn around. "I'm going to need them together on this one."

Frank's head dropped and his chest heaved a heavy sigh.

"But I *am* looking for new assistant," Zed added quickly. "It's not field work, but you get better dental."

Frank looked up and smiled, revealing a mouth full of rotten pug teeth.

Meanwhile, Jay led Kay into the top secret Tech

Unit. "The most advanced technologies from all over the universe are kept in this area," Jay explained.

Kay glanced around in awe at bizarre-looking machines, gadgets, and technology he couldn't begin to understand. "What's this?" he asked, reaching out to a holographic projection of a tiny planet. The miniature globe floated in the middle of a large metal box that seemed to keep it suspended in midair using some type of energy field.

"Don't touch that," Jay said casually, too involved with checking a series of readouts on another device to notice Kay poking his finger into a tiny ocean on the holographic planet.

Tiny ripples spread along the ocean lapping against three holographic continents on the globe.

At that same moment, fifty million light years away on a planet called Jarithia, a giant finger suddenly appeared in the sky. The massive finger dipped into Jarithia's ocean, creating a monstrous tidal wave which loomed above its largest city, poised to bury it under a flood of epic proportions.

"All is lost!" shrieked a Jarithian, racing through the city's streets. Seconds later, he and everything else was underwater.

Jay glanced at the globe, noticing the tiny ripple in its ocean. He glared at Kay.

"Nothing happened," Kay assured him, shrugging.

"Why don't you just keep your hands in your pockets while we're in here," Jay suggested.

Continuing through the Tech Unit, Jay reached a tall metal cabinet. He punched in a code known only to top-level security personnel, and flung open the cabinet's doors revealing an arsenal of weapons from around the universe.

Jay reached for the largest item in the cabinet—the Series Four De-Atomizer—the most powerful hand-held weapon known to the agents of Men in Black, and the weapon which Kay had carried during all his years as the organization's top operative.

Kay reached out for the De-Atomizer, but Jay pulled it back. Instead he handed his partner the tiny Noisy Cricket, a small pistol-shaped weapon Jay had been forced to use in his early days working under Kay's supervision.

"This is your signature weapon," Jay fibbed, as Kay took the Noisy Cricket, which looked like a toy ray gun, and stared at it disdainfully. "The one you used while I trained you."

"I took orders from you?" Kay asked in amazement.

"I taught you everything you know, sport," Jay replied, flashing a huge grin.

"Could we just get on with this?" Kay asked, shaking his head, anxious to regain his memory and learn the truth about his past.

"Not in that Cub Scout uniform, we can't," Jay quipped, pointing to Kay's U.S. Post Office outfit. "Let's get you some real clothes."

A few minutes later, following a quick visit to the outfitting department, Kay emerged in the standard Men in Black black suit with a white shirt, black tie, and black shoes. In fact, he was given the very same suit he had worn during his years with the agency.

"Now you look like you belong here," said Jay, leading his partner down a narrow hallway. They stopped in front of a door labeled DENEURALYZATION. "Right through here. That's where you get your marbles back."

As they stepped through the door, Kay noticed that the room looked like a large bowl, its clear walls of thick glass sloping toward a low circular point in the center of the floor. On the floor, next to the lowest point, sat a machine that looked like a cross between an electric chair and a one-man space capsule—the deneuralyzer.

"In a few minutes this machine will unlock information hidden deep in your brain," Jay explained in his most serious, dramatic voice. "That information might hold the key to Earth's very survival!"

Kay tugged at his shirt. "This collar itches," he said, clearly unimpressed by Jay's speech.

"Just get into the machine, will you?" Jay barked, pointing to the contraption.

Kay slipped into the deneuralyzer's seat. Jay adjusted

its metallic headpiece that rested on Kay's shoulders like a neck brace. "Ready?" he asked.

"You sure this thing's going to give me back my memories?" Kay asked.

"Yeah," Jay replied, adjusting a few dials on the machine. "That is if your advanced years haven't killed them already."

As Kay opened his mouth to respond, Jay shoved the mouthpiece in, silencing his partner and completing the final step in the procedure's setup.

Kay's deneuralyzation was about to begin.

CHAPTER 10

At the same time that Jay prepared Kay for de-neuralyzation, a long line formed in the customs and immigration area of Men in Black headquarters. This was where new arrivals from all over the universe passed through to begin their lives on Earth.

The line was populated by a menagerie of aliens. A ten-foot-tall, twelve-armed creature stood behind a small round blob of black goo. In front of the gooey alien stood a squat, reptilian being with four tails and no head.

At the front of the line Serleena approached a customs agent. Scrad stood behind her, with Charlie's head poking up from the backpack.

"Name and planet of origin?" the agent asked flatly.

For him, dealing with this odd gallery of life forms was simply another day on the job.

"Serleena Xath," the alien replied, still in her human form. "Planet Jorn. Kyloth System."

"Any fruits or vegetables?" the agent asked.

"Yes," Serleena said, pointing to Scrad and Charlie. "Two heads of cabbage."

"Reason for your visit?" the agent asked for the hundredth time that day.

"Education," Serleena replied, opening her coat to reveal her lingerie-clad body. "I want to learn to be a model. I'm told I have raw talent."

Overhearing this, all the customs agents in the room looked in Serleena's direction.

This was Scrad's cue. He dropped to the floor and rolled from side to side. "Help!" he shrieked. "Heart attack! Argg!" Charlie's eyes rolled back in his head, which dangled lifelessly next to Scrad's.

Scrad performed CPR, blowing air into Charlie's mouth while he banged on his own chest. Agents rushed to help the two-headed creature. That's when Serleena made her move.

Firing neural roots from her fingertips, she wove a dense web of muscle and nerves that paralyzed each agent it touched. Within minutes, the entire customs and immigration area was a tangled bramble of motionless Men in Black agents.

Scrad leaped to his feet and followed Serleena toward Zed's office.

From inside the body cavity of the dead alien in the nearby autopsy room, Frank lifted his slimy head and took in the aftermath of Serleena's attack. "Ah, jeez," he mumbled. "I think we're in trouble."

Seeing the aliens burst into his office, Zed rose slowly from his seat. Before he could say a word, Serleena wrapped her neural roots around his throat and lifted the Men in Black leader off his feet.

"Serleena, p—please," he stammered, struggling for breath.

Serleena tossed him to the floor. "It's been twenty-five years, Zed," she said, towering threateningly over his crumpled body. "I'm touched that you remember me."

"I never forget a pretty, uh, whatever that is," Zed replied, pointing to the neural roots extending from Serleena's fingertips. Zed lifted himself up into a seated position and reached for a panel of fifty red alarm buttons hidden beneath his desk. He quickly pressed the button labeled DENEURALYZATION.

At that very moment in the deneuralyzer room, Jay moved his finger toward the button which would switch on the machine. Loud alarms blared and Jay withdrew his hand. The doors slammed shut and the small circle at the low point on the floor opened revealing a long tube, about three feet wide, leading down into darkness.

"Breach!" Jay shouted, removing Kay's mouthpiece and headpiece, and helping him out of the de-neuralyzer. "Someone's infiltrated the building. Sorry, pal, but your memories are going to have to wait a little while longer."

"What's with the glass walls and the hole in the floor?" Kay asked, straightening his tie and tugging at his itchy collar.

"We're being flushed," Jay explained calmly.

"Flushed?" Kay asked.

"Ever been to a water park?" Jay asked.

Before Kay could answer, blue water filled the room, swirling around like a liquid tornado. The water swept the two agents into its flow, spun them around the room twice, then flushed them through the opening in the floor.

Whoosh!

Down they plunged, twisting through the corkscrew maze of underground pipes. Kay felt his cheeks being pulled up toward his forehead from the force.

Finally they were dumped out into two large tanks of water. Kay pushed open a hinged cover. Jay did the same in the tank next to Kay. Daylight streamed in as the two agents climbed from the tanks, their suits soaking wet.

Looking back at the tanks, Kay saw labels that

read NITROGEN. He realized that they were standing in the middle of Times Square. Giant video billboards flashed commercials as tourists streamed past them in packs, never even noticing the two dripping-wet men.

"Flushed," Jay repeated, wiping the water from his face.

"Got it," Kay replied.

"Look, I know this was a bad way to start, but you have to hang in there," Jay pleaded. "All I'm asking you to do—"

"—is save the world," Kay finished the sentence. "I save the world, and you tell me why I stare at the stars every night. I got it. Where to now, slick?"

"Hop in," Jay said, pressing a button on his key chain.

Kay looked around. "Hop in what?" he asked.

Jay's black sedan came screeching around the corner and squealed to a stop right in front of them, a Men in Black agent at the wheel.

"Who's that?" Kay asked.

"A friend," Jay replied, pressing another button on his key chain. The plastic "driver" deflated and folded up into the steering wheel's airbag compartment. "Can't have driverless cars tearing around the city, now can we?" He slipped in behind the wheel.

"That come standard?" Kay asked, climbing into the passenger seat.

Pulling out onto Broadway, Jay popped up a video

display in the middle of the dashboard. "Computer," he commanded. The monitor flickered to life. "Surveillance. Men in Black."

A series of images flashed across the monitor showing various sections of headquarters. Each picture showed a scene of destruction and devastation, the likes of which were unprecedented in the history of the organization. Serleena's neural netting encompassed agents and equipment, windows and doors, until the entire place looked like the aftermath of an attack by an angry spider—an incredibly huge angry spider!

When the monitor flashed an image of the autopsy room, something caught Jay's eye. "Computer, freeze," he ordered. "Now zoom in, camera six."

The image pulled in closer until it focused on the dead body. Jay spotted Frank's head peeking out from the opening. Jay punched a button on the monitor, sending a signal to a control panel in the autopsy room.

Beep! Beep! Beep!

Frank's head popped up from the alien. Grabbing a headset, he spoke quickly. "Jay, is that you? Where are you, partner?"

"We were flushed," Jay explained.

"Code 101," Frank reported. "Completely taken over."

"Who did it?" Jay asked.

"Some chick in leather, wearing a nightie," Frank replied.

"Stay where you are," Jay ordered. "I'll be in touch."

"Great," grumbled Frank, dropping back down into the alien's body. "I'll just stay where I am."

As Jay continued driving, Kay stared at a photograph he had pulled from his pocket. "What do you make of this?" Kay asked, holding the photo up. "I found it in my suit."

The image showed Kay at least twenty years younger. He was pointing at something that was not in the photo and smiling.

"Weird, huh?" said Kay, staring at the picture with absolutely no recollection of the time, place, or events leading up to its being taken.

"It's weird, all right," replied Jay. "You're smiling."

"That deneuralyzer at headquarters," Kay began, slipping the picture back into his pocket. "Is that the only one?"

"The only official one," Jay explained. "A couple of years ago the plans leaked out onto the Internet. Zed always thought that the odds were pretty good that some kid built one in his bedroom."

"So, what are we waiting for?" Kay asked.

"Good point," Jay conceded. "Computer. Internet."

The image on the screen shifted to the Men in

Black home page. "Ebay," Jay ordered, and instantly the screen shifted to the auction website. He typed in DENEURALYZER, and hit the enter key.

"Do you really think that—" Kay began.

"Just found it," Jay interrupted, as the words "Found 1 of 1 items: DENEURALYZER popped onto the screen. "Well, what do you know," Jay said, smiling as he read the seller's name at the bottom of the screen. "Look who has it. It's our old friend Jack Jeebs, the pawn shop king."

CHAPTER 11

In Men in Black headquarters, Serleena paced back and forth along a line of aliens who had been held in prison cells. Indeed they were the scum of the universe, the most vicious, ruthless criminals ever to show their faces, scales, horns, tails, and fangs on planet Earth.

Serleena had ordered Scrad and Charlie to free them all from their cells and bring them before her as volunteers for a mission to find and bring in Agent Kay.

Scrad scrambled up next to her. "Alien prisoners released and armed," Scrad announced when the last aliens had joined the motley crowd.

"Have you found Kay?" she asked.

"He's been neuralyzed," Scrad reported nervously,

looking down at his feet, then around the room, avoiding eye contact with his boss. "He's a civilian. No longer a Men in Black agent."

"What?" Serleena howled in rage. A few of the alien prisoners snickered at her outburst.

"See, he was here to get deneuralyzed," Charlie explained. "His memory's gone. So, he's not gonna remember what it is you need him to remember."

Serleena glared at Scrad and Charlie, her mind racing for a solution.

"But we'll find him," Scrad said quickly. "So please don't put anything in our ears!"

Serleena surveyed the line of prisoners again. She brought her fingertips together in front of her face and spoke. "Prisoners of the Men in Black, I'm short on time, so I'll make this simple. Whichever one of you brings Kay to me gets the Earth."

A low muttering spread down the line. Aliens laughed and slapped each other on the back.

"To find Kay," Serleena continued, "start by locating a deneuralyzer. His partner and he will be trying to get his memory back."

A tall, thick-armed alien spoke up. "I know a slimy creep named Jeebs who might have one of those," he growled.

Serleena pointed at Scrad and Charlie. "You lead this group," she ordered. "If you fail, I'm going to kill *you* and let *you* watch."

Charlie leaned in close to Scrad. "The first 'you,' that she said," he whispered. "Was that you or me? I was just wondering."

As the malevolent crew shuffled from the room, Serleena approached the last alien in line. He stood eight feet tall and was covered in a flowing black cape. Only his head was visible, and it appeared to be that of an elderly human man.

"Jarra," Serleena cooed. "Good to see you. It's a disgrace that they've kept a genius like you locked away in this sewer."

"That Eagle Scout, Agent Jay caught me siphoning Earth's ozone to sell on the black market," Jarra explained. "They're very touchy about the whole global warming thing."

"I need a spacecraft," Serleena announced. "Something that can travel three hundred times the speed of light. Certainly more powerful than anything they have here. Can you do it for me?"

"Of course, my old friend," Jarra replied. "Just give me Jay, and we'll call it even."

"Deal," Serleena agreed, nodding. Then she turned to a small alien robot that had been standing still since Scrad had led it into the room. "Gatbot, come with me. I have a special assignment for you."

The tiny robot lit up, its red and green lights flashing in its translucent midsection. It raised itself up several inches to reveal polished chrome wheels, then it rolled away following closely behind Serleena.

Jay pulled the black sedan over to the curb on a downtown street in front of an ancient-looking pawn shop. Kay glanced up as he stepped from the car and read the sign on the storefront, JEEBS' PAWN SHOP.

Jay entered first. The inside of the store was dusty and dingy. Long glass cases displayed old jewelry, cameras, and stereo equipment. At the sound of the door opening, a short man with a wrinkly face poked his head up from behind a counter.

"Hey, Jay," the man called, spotting the first agent entering the store. "Haven't seen you for a while. Sorry the store's such a mess, but since my business started booming on the Internet, I hardly even need a store anymore. How have you—"

The man behind the counter spotted Kay and stopped short. "Uh, oh!" he cried, ducking back down. "I heard that he retired. Listen Kay. I don't want any trouble."

"Shut up, Jeebs," Jay barked. "We need the de-neuralyzer."

Jeebs popped his head up again. "You're kidding? The great Kay's a neutral. Ha! I love it."

Kay stepped up to the counter and leaned in close to Jeebs. "Friend," he snarled. "You're standing between me and my memories. You got this thing or not?"

80

Jeff, a huge alien worm, lives in the New York subway system.

Jay uses a neuralyzer to erase the passengers' memories of Jeff.

Serleena interrogates Ben about the Light of Zartha.

Laura can't believe her eyes. Who are these strange creatures?

Zed tells Jay about the alien attack at the pizza parlor.

Frank gets his own Men in Black suit—he's finally official!

Jay asks Laura questions about what happened at the pizzeria.

Jay investigates Serleena's ship and reports back to Men in Black headquarters.

Jay explains to Kay that he is a former Men in Black agent, and that they need his help to save the Earth.

The post office workers are actually aliens!

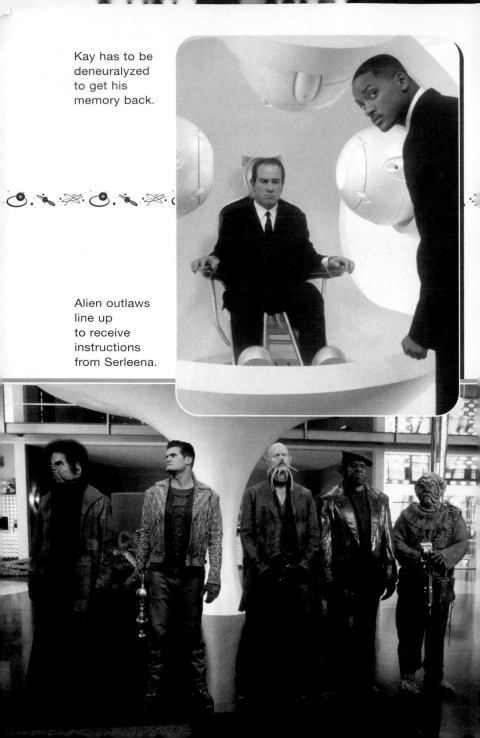

Kay has to be deneuralyzed to get his memory back.

Alien outlaws line up to receive instructions from Serleena.

Jay and Kay must fight to save the Men in Black from the evil Serleena.

Serleena tries to convince Kay to reveal the location of the Light of Zartha.

Scrad offers the proton detonator to Jay and Kay.

Jay and Kay watch the Light zoom home to Zartha.

"No," Jeebs replied stubbornly. "And even if I did, I'm in a lose-lose situation here. If it doesn't work, Kay dies, and you kill me," he explained to Jay. "If it does work I've brought back Kay, who'll hound me until my dying day."

Jay raised his Series Four De-Atomizer and pointed it at Jeebs' head. "Doesn't friendship count for anything?" he said, smiling.

Jeebs moved quickly to the cellar door and pulled it open. "I keep it downstairs," he admitted. "Right next to the snow blowers."

Jay and Kay followed Jeebs down the stairs. A few minutes later Kay was strapped into a homemade version of the high-tech marvel he had seen at headquarters. Pieces of old computers were held together by duct tape. Exposed wires ran around the chair's arms, connected to thin plumbing pipes.

"Ever use this thing?" Kay asked nervously.

"I used the exhaust fan once to make some hot-air popcorn," Jeebs replied, shoving a plastic piece from a snorkel into Kay's mouth. "But that's about it. Okay, have you removed all your jewelry?"

Kay nodded and grunted.

"Are you allergic to shellfish?" Jeebs asked.

Kay glared up at him.

"Okay! Okay!" Jeebs cried. "Let's go." He flipped the device's main switch.

Whirr! Whirr! WHIRR!

Power surged through the deneuralyzer, dimming the lights in the store as well as most of the lights in the neighborhood. Kay's eyes opened wide as fragments of past events flashed through his mind.

Only seconds had passed when Jeebs flipped off the machine's main switch.

WHIRR! Whirr! Whirr!

The deneuralyzer powered down, then went silent. Kay tumbled from the seat, crashing face first onto the floor. He twitched uncontrollably and smoke poured from his ears.

Jay kneeled close to Kay's body, which stopped moving. "Kay?" he asked softly. Getting no response, he stood back up.

"He's dead," Jeebs announced. "Oh, well."

Thoom!

Jeebs' head exploded into a million gooey fragments. Immediately, a new head started growing from his neck, expanding in size like a balloon inflating, until it was once again a full-sized head.

Kay got to his feet and slipped his Noisy Cricket back into his jacket pocket.

"Kay?" Jay asked tentatively. "Are you back? Did your memories return?"

"No," Kay said flatly.

"Then how did you know that his head would grow back?" Jay asked.

"I didn't," Kay explained. "I just don't like him."

"Oh, real nice," muttered Jeebs, making the final adjustments to his face.

"I'm outta here," Kay announced, heading up the cellar stairs. "Take care."

"Kay, wait!" Jeebs shouted up after him. "I just realized that I never got the updated software for this thing. Your brain needs to reboot! Give it a minute, for crying out loud!"

"Listen to him, Kay!" added Jay.

Kay ignored their pleading. He reached the top of the stairs, walked through the store, and vanished out onto the street.

Without warning, the back wall of the cellar tore open, shards of cinderblock and plaster dust exploded into the room. Through the gaping hole in the wall stepped an angry crew of heavily armed aliens, including the thick-armed alien who knew Jeebs. Scrad and Charlie brought up the rear.

"Where is he?" demanded Thick-Arms, referring to Jay, who had ducked behind the deneuralyzer.

"Over there," Jeebs replied, pointing to the spot where Jay crouched.

Thick-Arms lifted his weapon, and in one smooth motion blasted the deneuralyzer—and along with it, any hope of a second try at restoring Kay's memory. Jay stood up, his Series Four De-Atomizer trained on the group of intruders.

"Where's Kay?" Thick-Arms growled at Jeebs.

Before Jeebs could answer, Jay blasted his new head into putty, sending him staggering from the room.

An alien with a large bulbous nose and long thin arms grabbed Jay from behind, wrapping one arm around his throat, and grabbing the De-Atomizer with another. As the weapon left Jay's hand, it fired, blasting Thick-Arms.

"Where's Kay?" hissed the big-nosed creature, tightening his hold on Jay's windpipe.

Jay remained silent. The alien roared with rage then tossed him across the room. Jay crashed to the floor. His chin smacked into the grimy cement. Looking up, he found himself face-to-face-to-face with Scrad and Charlie.

"We really need Kay," Scrad said.

"He's a neutral," Jay groaned, slowly climbing to his feet. "He was neuralyzed."

"Tell us something we don't know!" screamed Charlie.

"Look, I'm not much for violence," Scrad explained. "But if I don't bring Kay back to Men in Black headquarters, a certain squiggly somebody is going to do me in. So where is he?"

"Don't know," Jay said defiantly, wiping the blood from his mouth.

"Bend him," Scrad ordered abruptly.

Before Jay had time to react, a seven-foot-tall,

muscular alien with huge gray arms grabbed him from behind. The powerful creature lifted Jay high over his head and pulled Jay's neck down toward his feet, bending his spine backward.

Jay grimaced in anguish, taking deep breaths, trying to meditate his way through the excruciating pain.

"I'll ask you one more time," Scrad barked. "Where is Kay?"

Jay closed his eyes, on the brink of passing out, then screamed in agony.

"AHHHH!"

CHAPTER 12

Kay wandered down the street in a daze. He had walked less than a block from the pawn shop in the dark when he noticed odd-looking people.

A mail carrier strolled by on his way home from work. Suddenly a green scaly tail popped out of his shorts. Kay looked on, wide eyed, as the postman tucked his tail back in and glanced around to make sure no one saw.

A homeless man pushed a shopping cart full of items collected from the street. Looking closely, Kay caught sight of two sets of glowing red eyes among the jumble of empty bottles and clothing. Four tiny orange hands, each with three fingers, reached out from the cart. The homeless man didn't seem to notice.

Kay's mind reeled, images from the past collided with the present. Looking down at the sidewalk, Kay spotted a cockroach staring up at him, fear showing in the little bug's eyes. Kay instinctively lifted his foot and prepared to bring his shoe down to squash the insect, when a door in his mind opened and a flood of memories came washing over him. He placed his shoe on the pavement next to the cockroach.

"Thanks," the little bug squeaked. "Real decent of you, friend."

Kay dropped his head back and took in the night sky. A broad smile spread across his face. The Men in Black's all-time greatest agent was back, memories and all.

Meanwhile, in the cellar of Jeebs' pawn shop, Jay teetered on the brink of unconsciousness.

"I think he's telling the truth," said Scrad. "He really doesn't know where Kay is."

"Then he's no good to us," grumbled the alien, tossing Jay to the floor.

"I'd like the honor of destroying the great Agent Jay," cackled an alien drooling from his shark-like mouth, yet standing on human-type legs. He aimed his weapon at the defenseless Jay, who struggled to his feet.

Thoom!

The shark-mouthed alien vaporized instantly, vanishing in a cloud of gray smoke. When the air cleared,

Kay stood over Jay, holding his Noisy Cricket. "Didn't I teach you anything, slick?" Kay quipped, looking down at his partner.

Recovering from the shock of Kay's blast, all the aliens in the room rushed right at him. A number of species had been discovered during Kay's time away from the Men in Black. Lifting himself painfully from the floor, Jay called out the weakness of each species as his partner swung into action.

"That's Gayroon, Kay," Jay yelled, pointing at the first alien to charge at Kay. "Hit him in the tendrils."

Kay grabbed two fleshy feelers growing from Gayroon's chin. He yanked hard, and sent Gayroon flipping across the room, reeling in confusion.

"That one's got a big eye on the top of his head!" Jay called out.

The next alien rushed forward, snarling and spitting. The two tiny eyes on its face glowed a sickly green. Its head was covered by a large, floppy cap. Kay tore the cap from the creature's head to expose a huge eyeball spread across its skull. Kay smashed his fist down hard onto the eye and sent the alien shrieking and stumbling away, clutching the top of his head.

"On your left!" Jay cried, referring to a skinny alien with two fleshy sacks dangling from his head. "Kick him in the—"

"Got it, champ," Kay shot back, unleashing a furious

roundhouse kick to the alien's rather obvious target.

A creature looking—and smelling—like dog poop appeared behind Jay. It spread its arms wide, intending to bring them together in one final, crushing blow.

"You need a partner, slick," Kay said when the last alien had been defeated.

"Had one," Jay replied, wiping the last bit of blood from his face. "Job got too tough for him. Now he delivers greeting cards."

"Well, I'm back," Kay said firmly. "Tuck your shirt in."

"Your memory's totally back?" Jay asked, staring into Kay's eyes.

"That's right," Kay replied.

"What's the Light of Zartha?" Jay asked.

"Never heard of it," Kay said, bounding up the stairs. "Let's get out of here."

Jay followed closely and in moments they were back out on the street in front of the pawn shop. "If your memory's back," he began as they reached the car, "how come you don't know about the Light of Zartha?"

"Must have neuralyzed myself," Kay explained. "To keep the information from me."

"Good plan," Jay said, shaking his head. They both reached for the handle on the driver's door.

"I drive," Kay announced.

"Yeah," Jay agreed. "A little blue van marked 'U.S. Mail'."

Kay shoved Jay out of the way and slipped into the driver's seat. "Get in," he ordered, nodding toward the passenger's seat. "And tell me where the scene of the crime is."

Jay stood outside the driver's door with his arms crossed, looking up to the sky. "I forgot where it is," he said. "Must have neuralyzed myself."

Kay sighed deeply. "You've become a real wise guy," he said, shifting over to the passenger's side.

"You taught me everything I know, slick," Jay replied as he slipped behind the wheel.

Jay sped through the Manhattan night, cutting between cars and dodging cabs, using the driving skills he had acquired during his days on the New York City police force. He filled Kay in on the little that he had already learned, including Serleena's destruction of Ben, and his own conversation with Laura.

"If you completed the investigation, why didn't you neuralyze her?" Kay asked, as they pulled up in front of Ben's Pizza.

"This is the scene of the crime," Jay said, ignoring his partner's question.

Jay and Kay entered the darkened restaurant. Kay immediately ducked down.

Whack!

Something cold, hard, and metallic bashed Jay in the face. He hit the floor hard. Kay aimed his Noisy

Cricket at the assailant and prepared to pull the trigger.

"No!" cried Jay, shoving Kay's arm down before he could get off a shot.

Laura stepped from the shadows holding a large round pizza tray. "I'm so sorry," she said glancing from Jay down to Kay. "I didn't realize it was you."

"This is Laura," Jay said as Kay put away his weapon. "Laura, this is my partner, Kay."

Kay nodded, walked quickly past Laura, and noticed a photograph on the wall. "This the Zarthan?" he asked, pointing at the man in the photo who stood next to a large fish he had apparently just caught.

"That's Ben," Laura explained. "You knew him?"

"Never saw him before," Kay replied.

"Wait a minute," Jay said, looking closely at the photo. "There's something familiar about the background . . . Where's that old photo of you?"

Kay pulled the photo from his pocket and handed it to Jay. He placed it next to the one of Ben. The two backgrounds matched precisely. They were now staring at a single picture of Ben with his arm around young Kay who was pointing to something not shown.

"So you neuralyzed yourself, then left yourself clues," Jay proposed.

"In case my replacement couldn't handle the situation," Kay explained.

"Maybe you shouldn't have created the situation in the first place," Jay shot back.

"Uh, boys," Laura interrupted, pointing to the photo. "Can we try to figure out what the clues mean?"

Kay looked at the wall next to the photo in the direction in which young Kay was pointing. It looked like he was pointing at an astronaut picture that was hanging on the wall across the room. Right next to the picture, a single key hung from a nail.

"Why didn't you just paint a sign on the wall that said, Kay's Secret Key?" Jay taunted his partner.

Kay snatched the key from the nail and looked at it closely. On one side it read "C18." Engraved on the back was GCT.

"Great," Jay said shaking his head. "Now all we have to do is figure out where—"

"I know where the key goes," Kay interrupted, as he pulled out his neuralyzer and pointed it at Laura.

"No!" Jay shouted, shoving Kay's arm down. "Not yet! I have a feeling she might be able to help me. I mean, help *us*!"

"Well she can't stay here," Kay pointed out, slipping the neuralyzer back into his pocket. "Sooner or later the Kylothians will be back here looking for clues."

Jay took Laura by the hand and led her from the pizzeria. "You can stay with some friends of mine," he offered.

"People like you?" she asked, slipping into the black sedan.

"Not exactly," Jay replied.

CHAPTER 13

Four aliens who looked very much like three-foot-tall earthworms shared a bachelor pad in lower Manhattan. Former Men in Black employees, the Worm Guys (as their coworkers at the organization called them) were currently on suspension from the agency, having been accused of stealing office supplies.

Restricted from being seen in public, the Worm Guys were basically trapped in their apartment, forced to entertain themselves.

When Jay, Kay, and Laura arrived at the Worm Guys' apartment, a party was in full swing.

"Jay!" all four Worm Guys shouted, when they caught sight of their favorite agent.

95

Jay saw one Worm Guy stretched out on a lounger reading *Travel & Leisure* magazine. Another lifted weights. A third sat on the couch, his eyes glued to the baseball game on TV, and the fourth was immersed in a hot tub, with a huge smile spread across his face.

"Listen, guys," Jay began. "Men in Black headquarters has gone Code 101—totally taken over. I need your help. I need you to keep Laura safe. This is Laura."

Laura stepped forward, stunned by the bizarre scene before her. She wasn't sure if she was more shocked by the fact that Jay's friends were talking worms, or by the disgustingly sloppy way in which they kept their apartment. "Hi," she said weakly, waving her hand.

"Wow!" all four worms shouted at once. "Hello, Lau-ra!"

"Why don't you sit over here?" the TV-watching worm suggested, patting the couch beside him.

"Shut up!" yelled the worm in the hot tub. "She'd rather slip into the tub with me."

"Oh, yeah, like you have a chance," called out the weight-lifting worm.

Kay stepped out from behind Laura. "They talk a lot," he whispered to her. "But they're harmless."

"I've dated worse," Laura whispered back.

"Kay!" the worms all shouted. "Glad to see you're back!"

Jay handed his communicator to Laura. "Call me if you need me," he said as he headed for the door. Then turning to the worms he added, "Take good care of her, guys. She's important to me."

All heads turned toward Jay.

"As a witness!" he shouted defensively. Then much to his surprise, Laura kissed him. Jay turned and walked from the apartment followed by Kay.

"Hey, Laura! You like games?" the magazine-reading worm shouted, leaning over and pulling a box from beneath his chair. "We've got Twister!"

"Twister!" the worms all shouted.

A short while later Jay followed Kay through Grand Central Terminal in midtown. It had a high arching marble ceiling that towered above the throng of people rushing to catch trains or get to appointments in the city.

"Why are we here?" Jay asked impatiently.

"GCT," Kay said. "Grand Central Terminal. Don't slow me down, rookie." When they reached locker C18, Kay slipped the key into the lock and popped the door open.

In his time as an agent of the Men in Black, Jay had seen some pretty wild things. But the sight that awaited him when the door to locker C18 swung open caught the seasoned agent by surprise.

An entire world filled with miniscule aliens existed

within the small metal locker. Some drove cars, some rode bikes, still others flew tiny planes. People moved among houses, cities—even mountain ranges and oceans—all inside the locker. The aliens who were going about their business stopped as the harsh light from the terminal flooded into their world.

"It's Kay! He's back!" the aliens of locker C18 shouted in unison. "All hail Kay, the life giver!"

"They think you're some kind of god!" Jay said, laughing and turning away.

"Nah, more like the Pope," Kay replied. "Good and gentle town-folk of locker C18, did I leave something with you for safekeeping?"

"Yes, O great and powerful Kay," replied a young alien. "The Time Keeper."

Kay reached into the locker and took an old digital watch—circa 1970—from a tall clock tower.

"Oh, no!" shrieked the aliens. "The precious Time Keeper is removed!"

"Here," said Jay, pulling off his watch and placing it on the clock tower. "Titanium case, waterproof to three hundred meters. Now you've got something with a little style."

"Who are you, stranger?" a young alien asked.

"Jay," he replied.

"All hail Jay!" the aliens shouted as a group.

"Was there anything else I left with you?" Kay asked, as Jay waved benevolently to his new subjects.

"Yes!" cried a weak craggy voice from inside the locker. Kay looked closely and spotted an elder of the community who stood upon a snowy mountaintop, his long white beard blowing in the breeze. "The commandments!"

"Yes!" cried a crowd who had gathered around the elder. "The Tablet!"

"We have lived by its words, and peace has reigned throughout our world," the elder explained. He handed Kay an old crinkled card, its edges torn and curling. "Pass it on to others so they too may be enlightened."

Kay took the card and looked at it closely. The wrinkled, worn piece of cardboard read TAPEWORM VIDEO. BLEECKER STREET. Below the store's name a series of rules were listed.

"All together now," the elder shouted.

"Be kind, rewind!" the aliens all chanted in unison.

"Go back and reconcile your past in order to move tranquilly into the future," the elder said, interpreting the first rule.

"Two for one every Wednesday!" the group chanted.

"Give twice as much as ye receive on the most sacred of days—every Wednesday," the elder explained.

Kay closed the locker door.

"So what's up with the video card?" Jay asked as

the two agents headed quickly though the terminal.

"Don't know," Kay replied tersely.

"What about the watch?" Jay asked, his patience growing thin.

"Don't remember," Kay replied softly.

"Take a wild guess, then," Jay said, exasperated.

Kay held out the watch. The digital numbers read: 59:37. Jay looked closely as the seconds counted down . . . 36 . . . 35 . . . 34. "I'm guessing that 59 minutes and 32 seconds is how long we've got to figure all this out," Kay stated, looking down at the video rental card. "Let's see if this place is still in business."

Returning to their car, the agents sped downtown. Scanning the storefronts on Bleecker Street, they soon found Tapeworm Video. When they entered the store, they were greeted by a sight almost as bizarre as the aliens of locker C18.

Rows of old, dusty shelves lined the walls, each one packed with videotapes. But instead of the usual categories—Comedy, Action, Drama—Jay and Kay saw labels for the Occult, the Bizarre, Conspiracies, and Oliver Stone films.

As odd as the offerings were, the customers were even odder. People shuffled among the aisles dressed in hooded sweatshirts and long trench coats. As Jay and Kay entered the store, the customers all looked away, as if not wanting to be recognized.

Behind the counter a young woman in her twenties, covered in tattoos and piercings, sorted through tapes. Kay stepped up and handed her the card.

"This card hasn't been used in a really long time," the clerk said, punching up the account on her computer. "Like, since before I was born."

"Been traveling on business," Kay explained.

"Ever been to Cambodia?" the clerk asked. "I hear that you can get a lobster dinner there for, like, a dollar!"

"No," replied Kay. "Can you tell us anything about the account?"

"Only that you never checked out a tape," the clerk replied. "You reserved one once, but you never picked it up." Then she called out "Newton! Come out here."

Out shuffled a guy wearing a T-shirt that read BEAM ME UP, SCOTTY. THERE'S NO INTELLIGENT LIFE ON THIS PLANET. His black-rimmed glasses were held together with electrical tape. Clipped to his belt was a button that read: THE X-FILES ARE TRUE! He clutched a bunch of tapes on UFO sightings.

"I'm Newton," he said. "I run the place." Then leaning in close to Jay and Kay he whispered, "Seen any aliens lately?"

"You need professional help, son," Kay said flatly.

"He's getting professional help," the clerk blurted out. "It's not working."

"The tape you reserved years ago," Newton said,

glancing around, unable to hide the conspiratorial tone in his voice. "Episode twenty-seven, the one about the Light of Zartha, right? I've got it upstairs."

Kay stared right into Newton's eyes. "Keep talking," he said firmly.

"You see, Hailey!" Newton shouted to the clerk. "I'm not paranoid. I was right. I knew it. These guys are the Men in Black!"

CHAPTER 14

At Men in Black headquarters, Serleena still had the place firmly in her grasp. Having severely punished Scrad and Charlie for failing to bring in Kay, she now turned her attention to Zed.

She grabbed him by the throat and lifted him into the air. "You tried choking me already," Zed wheezed, struggling for air. "It didn't work then, and it's not going to work now."

"Look at you, Zed," Serleena snarled, tightening her grip. "Twenty-five years later, still so handsome, so feisty. You know we both need the same thing. So call Kay and bring him here."

"I don't think so," Zed choked out.

"Listen," Serleena said. "Kay let his emotions get in

the way all those years ago, and now we have an unfortunate situation. But I need the Light, Zed."

"So you can exterminate an entire planet?" Zed wheezed.

"Zartha isn't *your* planet," Serleena pointed out. "But your planet is about to be destroyed because the Light is set to activate a fail-safe device if it isn't off this planet in less than an hour. So you see, old friend, if I lose, you lose. If I win, the Earth keeps spinning."

"All right, Serleena," Zed replied, gasping for breath. "You win. I'll call Kay."

The Men in Black chief set his communicator and handed it to Serleena, who placed the device next to her ear expecting to hear Kay's voice. Instead, she heard a recorded listing of the movies playing at a nearby multiplex theater.

This momentary distraction was all Zed needed. He grabbed a lamp from his desk and whacked Serleena, causing her to release her grip. Calling on reserves of energy and years of training, Zed did a triple back-flip, then bounded up the curved glass wall of his office. Gathering momentum and using gravity to add to the force, Zed unleashed a powerful kick to Serleena's head.

She blinked once, then smiled, completely shaking off the effects of the kick. "So very feisty still," she said, laughing. "It's just unfortunate that your planet will soon cease to exist and it will be your fault."

Moving with blinding speed, Serleena lashed out at Zed, knocking him out cold. Serleena glanced down through Zed's window to the main level. She spotted Frank in the autopsy room, poking his head out of the dead alien's body.

"Bring me that creature!" she screeched at Scrad. "NOW!"

Jay, Kay, Newton, and Hailey stepped into Newton's room. Although well into his thirties and the manager of a video store, Newton still lived with his parents. Jay saw that the room was packed with posters from science fiction movies, newspaper clippings about UFOs, model spaceships, and other paraphernalia of a man obsessed with aliens.

Just our type, Jay thought as he watched Newton sort through his huge videotape collection. Each tape was carefully labeled, alphabetically filed, and exhaustively crossreferenced by subject, actor, and year.

"Here it is!" Newton announced triumphantly. He handed the tape to Jay.

Jay scanned the label on the tape's spine. "*The Mystery of the Light of Zartha*," he read aloud. "Narrated by Peter Graves. Finally, some hard evidence," Jay said sarcastically, and he handed the tape back to Newton who popped it into the VCR.

Corny, screechy, mysterious music blared from the TV's speaker, then Peter Graves strolled onto a cheesy set. Ratty rec-room furniture was surrounded by backdrops showing paintings of distant planets. The backdrops shook with each step Graves took. Clasping his hands together seriously, he looked right at the camera and spoke: "Although no one has been able to prove their existence, a quasi-governmental agency known as the Men in Black supposedly carries out secret operations here on Earth in order to keep us safe from aliens throughout the galaxies. Here is one of their stories that 'never happened,' from one of their files that 'doesn't exist'."

Newton looked over at Jay and Kay who remained riveted to the screen. A piece of black construction paper splattered with white dots filled the screen—a weak attempt to portray the vast night sky.

Peter Graves continued: "Nineteen seventy-eight. The devastating War of Zartha had raged on for fifty years. The good and pure Zarthans had been brought to the brink of destruction by their enemies, the evil Kylothian invaders."

A cheap prop representing the big bad Kylothian spaceship spun in front of the cardboard starfield.

"Sparkles on a Frisbee," Jay mocked the cheap re-creation. "Scary!"

The narration droned on: "But despite the gloomy outlook, the Zarthans had a great treasure, the Light of Zartha. This was a source of power so awesome, it alone could mean victory and restoration for the Zarthans . . . or complete annihilation if it fell into the hands of the Kylothians.

"A decision was made to hide the Light on an insignificant blue planet, third from the sun. A group of Zarthans made the journey to Earth, led by the Keeper of the Light—"

"Lauranna," Kay whispered, his eyes opening wide as a long buried memory suddenly resurfaced.

"Princess Lauranna," Peter Graves confirmed.

All eyes in the room turned to Kay who stared at the screen as if in a trance. The story went on: "Lauranna begged the Men in Black to help her hide the Light on Earth, but they could not intervene."

At this point the video cut to a cornfield drenched in bright sunshine. Actors portraying Zarthans, Kylothians, and Men in Black agents stood in the field.

"No," Kay blurted out, the memories flooding back in a torrent. "That's wrong. It was night. And it was raining." Kay no longer saw the images on the TV screen. His mind filled with the terrible events of twenty-five years ago, events in which he played an integral part.

He stood in a field at night, as rain poured down. Before him, Serleena moved menacingly closer. She hadn't taken on a human form back then, and so a hooded mass of neural roots approached Kay, young once again in his memory.

"You've been wise not to hide the Light, Agent Kay," Serleena said in an unearthly voice.

"Kay, please, I beg you," cried a woman next to him. "Don't let them have it!"

Kay turned to the beautiful Princess Lauranna of Zartha. Rain ran down her face like endless tears. "If they have the Light, it will mean the end of our entire civilization."

Another agent spoke up. "Princess, if we offer you protection, we jeopardize the Earth," he explained. "I'm afraid we have no choice. The rules on this are clear. We must remain neutral."

Serleena stepped right up to Kay. "Where is it?" she snarled.

"You didn't think we would just give it you?" Kay replied, smirking. "We're neutral. You want it. Go get it!"

A thunderous roar filled the field, followed by a blinding flash of red and orange as a rocket blasted from a silo behind them. The ship tore across the night sky heading for space. Serleena unleashed a horrifying bellow. "No!!" she shrieked.

Serleena raced to her nearby spaceship, grabbed a weapon, and fired—striking Lauranna with a direct hit.

"Lauranna!" yelled Kay, as the princess fell into his arms.

Serleena slipped into her ship and blasted off, vanishing into the night. Men in Black agents fired at the ship as she sped away.

Kay cradled Lauranna's lifeless body in his arms. He unclenched his fist revealing a silver charm bracelet with a white stone in its center which the princess had handed him moments before she died.

As Kay relived the actual events in his mind, the others had to make do with the video's reenactment. Still, they all got the gist of the story.

Peter Graves wrapped it up: "Never knowing it even happened, the people of Earth were once again saved by a secret society of protectors known as the Men in Black."

Kay reached out and stopped the tape. "I shouldn't have done that," he sighed, the full impact of his recovered memories hitting home.

"You didn't send it off the planet," Jay guessed. "That rocket was just a decoy to keep Serleena chasing around the galaxy. You hid it here. That was always your plan with Lauranna."

"I went off book," Kay stated. "I broke the rules."

Kay turned and saw Newton and Hailey holding hands and brushing back tears.

"That's so sad," Newton moaned.

"It's so beautiful," Hailey added. "You risked everything for the woman you loved!"

Kay looked quickly at Jay, as one more memory popped into his head. "The bracelet!" he announced. "Laura's wearing the charm bracelet. She's in danger. Got to contact the Worm Guys!"

Jay nodded and pulled out his neuralyzer. He and Kay slipped their dark glasses on as Jay pointed the device at Hailey and Newton, then pressed a button.

Flash!

Their minds went vacant for a second, all memory of the Men in Black was erased. Newton stared blankly ahead waiting to be told what to do next. Jay leaned in close to him.

"Take her out for a nice lobster dinner," he said, nodding toward Hailey. Then the two agents bolted from the room.

CHAPTER 15

At the Worm Guys' apartment, Laura was enjoying another game of Twister. The four worms bent into a number of positions, and Laura was right there in the middle, playing along.

She was about to spin for her next turn when the communicator that Jay left with her beeped wildly. "Hello?" she said when she flipped the device open.

"Laura, it's me," Jay's voice blared through the speaker.

"Oh, hi, Jay," Laura replied. "We're playing Twister. These guys are really good at it. I guess it's because they don't have spines."

"Laura, listen to me," Jay said forcefully. "Are you wearing a charm bracelet?"

"Yes," she replied, looking down at the bracelet

dangling from her wrist. A small charm in the shape of a pyramid hung from the delicate chain.

"Is it glowing?" asked Jay.

"Yes, and it's never done that before," she replied.

"Laura, don't let that bracelet out of your sight," Jay pleaded. "We're on our way over there."

"Could this be the Light of Zartha?" she wondered.

Back in the Men in Black sedan, Jay finished his call with Laura and quickly punched in another number.

A red light on his car communicator flashed, indicating that the call had gone through. "Frank, listen," Jay spoke rapidly. "We're on our way to the Worm Guys' apartment. See if you can get to the Sub Control Panel and deactivate the lockdown. We'll be there as soon as we can."

Jay switched off the communicator without waiting for an answer, knowing that Frank had to be careful not to be discovered.

At Men in Black headquarters, Serleena switched off Frank's communicator and laughed. "Nice of your friends to tell us where they're headed," she cackled. Frank, who was bound and gagged, was lying on the floor of Zed's office next to his boss, grumbling and growling. "Scrad! Go to the apartment."

Back in the car, Kay snapped out of his own thoughts long enough to give Jay a hard time. "Why didn't you say 'I love you'?"

"I don't even like Frank," Jay replied, knowing full well what Kay meant.

"I'm talking about Laura," Kay corrected him. "You're sweet on her, and as long as you're in the Men in Black, that's a mistake."

"You're nuts," Jay snapped back.

"It's why you didn't neuralyze her after your first interview," Kay continued. "You got soft."

"Like you did with Lauranna?" Jay asked.

"I put our entire planet in danger by going off book," Kay admitted. "Don't go soft on me, kid. We can't afford it."

By the time Jay and Kay reached the Worm Guys' apartment, it was too late. The door had been kicked in. They were greeted by the devastating remains of what looked like a war zone. The TV had been blown into a million fragments. The hot tub had a huge hole in its side and water had flooded everywhere. The couch was a smoldering ruin. There was no sign of Laura.

"Laura!" Jay called out. He received no answer.

"Over here," Kay shouted from across the wreckage of the living room. Scattered around the room were the Worm Guys—all cut in half.

"Neeble, is that you?" Jay asked one Worm Guy whose lower half was ten feet away.

Neeble looked down, realizing that half his body was missing. Glancing at his lower half, he saw a pair

113

of eyes open, as the severed piece became a new worm. All around the room, the same thing was happening to the others.

"Geeble? Sleeble? You guys gonna be okay?" Jay asked the others.

"No problem, Jay," Geeble replied, staring at his lower half which now stood up and brushed itself off. "Twice as many worms is twice as much fun!"

"Who did this?" Jay asked, helping a few of the worms to their feet.

"Some dumb two-headed guy burst in and started blasting everything," Sleeble explained. "He was in a real hurry, but he stopped to catch the end of *Everybody Loves Raymond*. Then he blew up the TV."

"Where did they take Laura?" Jay asked impatiently.

"Men in Black headquarters," Sleeble said. "They're going to use an impounded ship to go back home with the Light."

Kay led Jay and the worms to an apartment located across the street from Men in Black headquarters, where a family was sitting on the couch watching TV.

Thoom!

Kay kicked open the apartment door and rushed into the living room, followed closely by Jay and the Worm Guys.

"Don't worry folks," Kay said in as friendly a voice

as he could manage. "I used to live here and I left a few things."

As the family stared in stunned silence, Kay slid open a panel on the far wall of the living room and pressed a small button. The wall rose up like a curtain in a movie theater, revealing a secret room filled with high-tech weapons.

Kay dashed into the secret room and tossed weapons out to Jay and the Worm Guys. "Lock and load, baby!" shouted Neeble, as the other worms whooped it up. During their time as active Men in Black agents, the worms had worked as accountants. The whole concept of carrying weapons and saving the planet was new to them, and they were enjoying every second.

Kay emerged from the room with a duffle bag filled with additional weapons and equipment. He pressed the button on the wall and slid the panel shut. As the wall was lowered back down, closing off the secret room, Jay and Kay put on their sunglasses. Then Jay pulled out his neuralyzer and pointed it at the family.

Flash!

All memory of the agents and the secret room was purged from their minds.

"You will love and cherish each other for the rest of your lives," Jay said, planting the suggestion into their receptive brains. "And your daughter," said Jay, pointing to the young girl on the couch, "should be able to stay up as late as she wants, and eat cookies, and candies, and stuff."

The small, heavily-armed strike force of men and worms assembled in front of the entrance to Men in Black headquarters. The Worm Guys, caught up in the spirit of battle, strapped ammo belts across what passed for their chests, painted camouflage makeup on their faces, and gripped weapons in each hand. Although they looked the part, they were thoroughly unprepared for the formidable foes they were about to encounter.

"You guys ready?" Jay asked.

"Yes, sir!" the worms all shouted. "Looking for a few good worms, sir!"

"Cut that out, will you?" Jay said as he lifted a massive bazooka and aimed at the front door. "Okay, here we go!"

"No, wait!" shouted Kay, but not in time.

Ka-thooom!!

Jay blasted the front door into scrap metal. "Wait for whaaaaa—" Jay yelled as the pressurized entryway sucked the agents into the building, followed by a swirl of leaves, papers, and a hot dog cart left on the sidewalk.

Jay, Kay, and the worms crashed in a pile of arms, legs, worm bodies, and garbage at the far end of the hallway.

"Wait for depressurization!" Kay screamed. "That's what! Code 101 lockdown. Nothing comes in, nothing goes out. Did you sleep during orientation, rookie?"

Untangling themselves from each other, two men and a bunch of worms—representing planet Earth's best and only hope for survival—raced for the elevators.

CHAPTER 16

On the rooftop launchpad of Men in Black headquarters, the alien known as Jarra was finishing up work on a spaceship for Serleena to use to escape from Earth. All around him lay dozens of dismantled spacecraft, from which he had taken parts for his incredibly fast and maneuverable creation.

Inside the spaceship Laura was strapped to a seat, awaiting her journey with Serleena to Zartha where she would be forced to witness the destruction of a world.

Jarra attached the last few components, turned off his welding torch, and spoke into a nearby video communications monitor.

"Serleena, we're ready," he announced.

Fifteen floors below in Zed's office, Serleena saw

Jarra's face on a video screen. "I'm on my way," she said, switching off the monitor.

Serleena turned to Scrad. "The one regret I have about getting the Light off this planet is that it will save the Earth from destruction," Serleena said as she handed Scrad a metal globe about the size of a grapefruit. "This is a proton detonator. Once I'm gone, set it and make the Men in Black headquarters disappear."

Then she strode from the office, leaving Scrad staring down at the powerful explosive device in his hand.

The elevator doors slid open onto the main hall of the Men in Black headquarters. Instantly, automatic weapon fire strafed the inside of the elevator car with a barrage of bullets. The tiny robot called Gatbot fired round after round of ammo into the car.

Anticipating Serleena's strong defense, Jay, Kay, and the Worm Guys clung to the ceiling of the elevator car as bullets shredded the walls just below them.

"Get to the launchpad on the roof!" Kay told Jay.

"Okay, Worm Guys," Jay yelled, preparing to make a mad dash for the roof elevator. "Give me cover!" Jay glanced over at the worms who, despite their fearsome appearance, were now trembling in terror.

"T—T—Too scared!" stammered Sleeble. "C—Can't move."

Jay shook his head. "Accountants with guns," he muttered.

"I'll give you cover," Kay shouted. "Go!"

Kay leaned down, extended his weapon out the elevator's doorway, and blasted at Gatbot. Startled by the attack, the tiny alien robot backed off.

Jay dropped to the ground, sprinted across the hall, and fired his bazooka at Gatbot. He reached the small elevator which led to the roof and slipped inside. Gatbot shifted position and emptied a round in Jay's direction, just as the elevator doors slid shut.

"Worms, listen up!" Kay ordered, once again flattening himself against the elevator's ceiling. "Get down to Sub Control Panel 7 R Delta. Shut down all power to the building. That way even if Jay can't stop them, they won't be able to launch."

Sleeble shook his head. "T—Too scared!" he stuttered. "Can't do what Jay did."

Kay yanked open a hatch in the elevator's ceiling and pointed up into the darkness above.

"Oh," said Geeble, the relief apparent in his voice. "That way. *Away* from the bullets. No problem. Okay, worms, move 'em out!" Geeble led the worms up through the hatch and into the narrow elevator shaft.

Kay spotted Gatbot rolling toward him. He pulled a grenade from his belt, punched the DOOR CLOSE button, swung up and out of the elevator car, and tossed the grenade back in just as Gatbot entered the car.

Thoom!

The grenade detonated behind the closed door destroying both the elevator car and the tiny robot.

Standing in the main hall, Kay breathed a quick sigh of relief, then turned and ran right into Serleena.

"Nice to see you again, Kay," she cooed. Neural roots extended from her fingers and wrapped around his neck.

"I should have taken care of you when I had the chance," Kay said.

Serleena yanked him by the neck and slammed him into a wall. "You wouldn't be in this mess if you had done what you were told," she snarled. "And she'd still be alive. You did love Lauranna, didn't you?"

Boiling with rage, Kay reached out to grab Serleena by the throat, but his hand passed right through her thin shell of human-looking skin. A thicket of neural roots poured from the opening, spreading over Kay's body.

The doors to the roof elevator slid open and Jay darted toward the spaceship that had been moved into launch position.

"Launch in four minutes," a computer-generated voice announced over a loudspeaker.

Jay climbed up into the ship and saw Laura struggling

against the straps that held her. "Laura!" he cried. "Are you all—"

A powerful metal tentacle grabbed him from behind, yanked him from the ship, and sent him sprawling onto the launchpad. Jay looked up and saw Jarra hovering several feet off the ground.

"Jarra," Jay replied casually, slowly getting to his feet. "You're cruising around smoothly these days."

"I was bored," Jarra explained. "Had a little time to tinker down in isolation."

Dropping his cape to the ground, Jarra exposed the lower half of his body which was actually a shiny metal flying saucer. The organic top half of his body rested on the saucer that had powerful metal tentacles extending from it.

A door on the saucer suddenly slid open. Six miniature versions of Jarra—half organic, half flying saucer with tentacles—flew out, hovering menacingly around big Jarra. "A paper clip here, a piece of wire there," he said casually. "You know, tinkering."

Jarra lashed out at Jay with a tentacle, sending him stumbling backward.

"I need to take the girl with me," Jay stated firmly.

"Over our dead titanium bodies," Jarra cackled.

The six tiny Jarras spun rapidly, their small but dangerous tentacles outstretched. Moving into formation, they converged and closed in on Jay.

The whirling saucers battered Jay on all sides. Jay

squatted and grabbed a piece of metal pipe left over from one of the ships Jarra had dismantled.

Jay swung the pipe wildly, sending the mini-Jarra saucers backing away. One saucer zipped in, trying to grab Jay's leg. He bashed the tiny disc, sending it spinning out of control. It slammed into a wall and dropped to the floor, damaged beyond repair.

The remaining saucers formed a circle around Jay, darting in and out, keeping him off balance as he tried to defend himself.

"Kill me," Jay offered. "Let the girl go."

"Such a deal," Jarra replied, smiling.

One of the minisaucers caught Jay on the ankle, wrenched his leg out from under, and sent him crashing to the ground with a thud.

"Launch in ninety seconds," the computer voice boomed.

As Jay scrambled to his feet, two of the mini-saucers converged, snatching his arms with their tentacles, and tossed him into the side of a dismantled ship.

"I'd like to see you two try that again," Jay shouted, setting his feet and bracing himself against the ship.

As if on command, the two minisaucers zoomed at Jay from opposite directions. Timing his jump perfectly, Jay leaped straight up into the air. The two saucers collided and exploded in a tiny orange fireball.

Jay saw Jarra leading the remaining minisaucers in an all-out rush toward him. They flew in a triangular formation, the razor claws on the ends of their tentacles extended.

"I want him in pieces!" Jarra raged as the formation closed in on Jay.

Jay reached out and grabbed the damaged saucer, then flung it like a Frisbee at the charging formation.

"Launch in fifteen seconds," the computer announced.

The spinning saucer careened off of Jarra, knocking him into the smaller versions of himself, which collided with each other and exploded into tiny flaming fragments.

Jay quickly freed Laura, then flipped some switches on the launchpad's control panel.

"Launch aborted," came the announcement over the loudspeaker.

Meanwhile Jarra struggled to free himself from the tangle of spaceship parts he had landed in. Fuel leaked from a large hole in the bottom of his saucer. "Take the girl," Jarra offered. "But let me go."

Jay shrugged. "Such a deal," he said as he kicked a glowing welding torch into the pool of fuel gathering on the ground. The fuel ignited and flames traveled along its trail, racing up into Jarra's saucer.

Foom!

Jarra exploded in a shower of sizzling metal.

"Paper clip here, piece of wire there," Jay repeated as he and Laura raced from the rooftop.

The Worm Guys crawled through the ventilation shaft, making their way toward the control center.

"Approaching the J5 intersection," Geeble reported into his communicator. "We're right above Sub Control Panel 7 R Delta, Kay. Kay?"

Geeble heard only static.

Sleeble heard the clicking of tiny feet racing along the top of the metal vent above them. Then a dozen heavily-armed alien crickets poured into the shaft from a small opening in the vent and opened fire on the worms.

The worms returned the fire, which bounced crazily around the confined space. But the worms were outnumbered and soon found themselves over-whelmed.

"Retreat!" ordered Geeble, and the worms raced toward the end of the shaft. Trapped with their backs against the wall and the crickets making a final charge, the worms unleashed a plan.

All at once the worms split themselves in half. As each new half came to life, its top portion tossed it a weapon. Within seconds, the crickets were greatly outnumbered. They dropped their weapons and ran from the vent shaft.

"Worms rule! Worms rule! Worms rule!" they

chanted, as they resumed their march to Sub Control Panel 7 R Delta.

Back in the main hall, Kay was down to his last few breaths—the tangled web of Serleena's neural roots were choking him.

"I have to run, Kay," Serleena announced, tightening her grip on his neck and chest. "But before I squeeze you like a tube of toothpaste, the last thing I want you to think about is all the destruction that's about to happen because of your stupidity."

"It didn't happen then," Kay wheezed. "And it's not going to happen now."

"You can't stop us!" Serleena boasted. "We're born conquerors."

"I'll give you one last chance to surrender, you slimy Kylothian invertebrate," Kay snarled, his voice barely above a whisper.

"What are you going to do to stop me?" Serleena asked, laughing.

"Not me," Kay replied, pointing up. "Him."

High above, Zed peered down from his office. Frank had managed to chew through his ropes, then Zed's, freeing them both. Zed dropped a gun toward the main floor where Jay now stood behind Serleena, Laura by his side.

Jay caught the gun and aimed it at Serleena. "Your flight's been canceled," he said, pulling the trigger.

Poom!

The noise from the gun bounced around the cavernous main hall. The shot it fired blasted Serleena into a thousand squiggly pieces.

CHAPTER 17

Jay flashed the thumbs-up sign to Zed, who returned the gesture. Frank, standing by his boss's side, added a paws-up. "You all right?" Jay asked Kay, who was leaning against the wall, rubbing his throat.

Kay nodded. At that very second, the lights went out.

Down at Sub Control Panel 7 R Delta, the Worm Guys let out a huge cheer.

"We did it!" shouted Geeble. "We cut the power and saved the Men in Black!"

"Worms rule! Worms rule!" they chanted again.

Back on the main floor, Jay fumbled in the darkness for his car keys. "Worms," he muttered, shaking his head and laughing. He pulled the keys from his pocket and pressed a button on the key chain. The sleek black sedan rolled into the main hall.

"Talk about service," Laura said, staring wide-eyed as the inflatable driver collapsed into the steering column.

"I need the bracelet, Laura," Jay explained, heading for the driver's door.

"I'm going with you," Laura insisted.

"Laura, please," Jay said.

"She's coming with us," Kay announced, moving around to the driver's side. "Everybody in."

Jay shrugged, handed the keys to Kay, then scooted around to the passenger side.

With Kay behind the wheel, Jay beside him, and Laura in the backseat, the Men in Black sedan sped from the main hall down into a secret tunnel. Picking up speed, the car raced up a hidden ramp, bounded out onto the street, and screeched off into the Manhattan night.

Back in a dark corner of the main hall, one tiny section of neural root pulsed and shook. Serleena still lived—and now began to grow!

As the sedan raced through the streets, Kay reached one arm into the backseat and took Laura's hand. "May I?" he asked, looking at her glowing charm bracelet.

"It's telling us the departure point," he explained.

Jay and Laura looked closely at the small pyramid-shaped charm dangling from the bracelet.

"That's only half the story," Kay continued, increasing

his speed and checking his digital watch. "Not only does the bracelet tell us the departure point, it also activates a fail-safe device. If we don't get the Light off this planet in exactly eleven minutes and fifteen seconds, Earth goes bye-bye. The good news is, the Kylothians won't get the Light. The bad news is, you won't be able to use those courtside Knicks tickets for next week's game, as neither you nor the court will exist."

Whomp!

Something rammed into the back of the car, sending Kay, Jay, and Laura jolting forward.

"What?" Kay exclaimed, turning around quickly.

He spotted the sleek spaceship which Jarra had built for Serleena speeding along behind them in close pursuit. Serleena piloted the ship.

Kay turned the wheel hard to the left, tires squealing as he whipped around a corner. Serleena followed closely, smoothly making the turn, gaining on the speeding sedan.

Kay looked down at the little red button on the steering column. Recalling that the button transformed his old Men in Black car into a speedy flying machine, he punched the button without saying a word.

"Wait!" screamed Jay.

"Don't worry, I know what I'm doing, slick," Kay said calmly.

The car took off as if it had been shot from a cannon, accelerating down the street at blinding speed. The dashboard—including the steering wheel—vanished. Heat-resistant panels emerged, forming an outer skin which covered the entire exterior. The sedan now looked more like a miniature space shuttle than a car.

"You've kicked it into hyperspeed!" Jay shouted.

"Where's the steering wheel?" Kay asked looking at the smooth, blank dashboard.

"At hyperspeed you need to fly it using the navigational stalk," Jay replied as he flipped a small switch under the dashboard.

A super high-tech control panel popped from the dash right in front of Kay, pinning him to his seat. The panel looked like an oversized video-game controller, complete with a joystick.

Kay grabbed the navigational stalk and pulled hard to the left. The car sped around a corner, doing a complete three-hundred-and-sixty-degree roll, tossing the three passengers around the inside like rag dolls.

"The triggers operate the right and left movements," Jay explained to Kay as he tried to untangle himself from Laura. "The toggle switch handles the stabilizers and rudder."

"Oh," Kay said casually, hitting a switch. The car

flipped upside-down, sending Laura tumbling onto Jay.

"If we die," Laura began, looking right into Jay's eyes. "I want you to know you're the only person I ever loved."

"Really?" Jay said. "That's amazing. I feel the same—"

Blammm!

A torpedo slammed into the back of the sedan. It burst into flames and spun out of control.

"I'll get back to you on that," Jay said to Laura as they strained to regain their balance in the spinning, flaming car. He punched a button on the car's communication system. "Worms!" he yelled. "We need you!"

In the main hall of Men in Black headquarters, the Worm Guys were busy celebrating, swapping stories about their heroic mission with Frank, who held court with some tall tales of his own.

"So I said to her," Frank boasted, "'Listen, you pile of squirmy guts, if you don't want me to kick your skinny Zone Diet butt, you'd better—'"

"WORMS!" Jay's voice blared from a nearby speaker.

"Jay?" Sleeble replied into the speaker.

"Where are you guys?" Jay shouted.

"Uh, just cleaning up," Sleeble lied. "You know, helping Zed."

"I need you at the main Men in Black computer!" Jay ordered. "Now! We've lost control of the vehicle. We're being fired on. Kay pressed the red button. The main computer can lock onto and destroy the ship that's attacking us. I'll walk you through the routine."

Sleeble looked up at the huge, egg-shaped monitor above his head. On the screen it read COMPUTER SHUT DOWN IMPROPERLY. RE-CONFIGURING HARD DRIVE. 7 MINUTES REMAINING . . ."

"Uh-uh, Jay," Sleeble stammered nervously. "When we shut off the power before, we may have done something to the computer. You couldn't stand by for about seven minutes, could you?"

Frank grabbed the microphone from the worm's hand. "Jay, it's Frank," he said, choking back tears. "You were the best darn partner a Remoolian could ever have. I'm gonna miss you, pal." Then Frank switched off the communicator.

Jay shook his head in disbelief. "He hung up on me," he muttered.

"I've got an idea," said Kay. He pressed the auto-pilot button.

Fooosh!

The inflatable pilot burst from an opening in the floor and ended up in Kay's lap, its under-inflated plastic head dangling to one side.

"Autopilot doesn't work with hyperspeed!" Jay barked.

"I could really use a steering wheel!" Kay screamed back.

Jay shoved both Kay and the inflatable pilot out of the way, slipping into the driver's seat and grabbing the navigational stalk. "Didn't your mama ever buy you a Game Boy?" he yelled, pulling hard on the stalk and gaining control of the speeding sedan.

Behind them, Serleena fired another torpedo from her ship.

"Hang on!" Jay shouted, moving the stalk with a subtle flick of the wrist. The sedan turned sharply to the right as the torpedo exploded in the air.

Looking down at lower Manhattan, Jay spotted the entrance of a subway station. "I have an idea!" he shouted. "Hang on. We're going straight down!"

"No!" cried Laura. "Straight down is bad! It's idiotic!"

The car dove down, plunging like a stone. On the street, tourists and businesspeople shrieked in terror, diving out of the way and cursing at the streaking vehicle.

Laura squeezed her eyes shut as Jay pulled back lightly on the stalk.

Swooping into the entrance of the Chambers Street subway station, the car flew down the stairs, then banked sharply to the right, entering the subway tunnel. It soared through the tunnel flying right above the track.

Serleena followed, diving into the subway, navigating the narrow twisting tunnel, all the time gaining on the car.

"Lights!" Jay cried, squinting into the darkness ahead. Responding to his voice command, the car's headlights flashed on, lighting the track and tunnel before them. Unfortunately, the lights also made them an easy target.

Baamm!

Serleena bashed into the back of the car, sending it skidding against the tunnel wall. Sparks sprayed in all directions.

"The subway doesn't seem like the best place to lose her," Kay pointed out.

"Where is he?" Jay hissed through clenched teeth.

"He?" Laura asked. "You're looking for a 'he' down here?"

Something large and round appeared vaguely ahead, like another tunnel moving toward them.

"HE!" shouted Laura. "Who's he?"

"Tighten your seatbelts, gang. And hang on," Jay ordered. Then he shut down the throttle. The car stopped suddenly and dropped onto the subway tracks with a scraping clang, wrenching its passengers forward against their seatbelts . . .

At that moment, Jeff, the giant subway alien, loomed huge in their headlights. He opened his gigantic jaws wide, filling the entire height of the tunnel. Then he licked his lips with his thick, craggy tongue.

"Yaaaiiii!" shrieked Serleena, unable to stop her spaceship from flying right into Jeff's gaping jaws. He slammed his mouth shut and swallowed the ship. With a satisfied wave of his enormous tail, Jeff disappeared back into the darkness of the tunnel.

CHAPTER 18

The Men in Black sedan screeched to a bumpy landing on a downtown rooftop overlooking the Statue of Liberty. Kay, Jay, and Laura jumped from the car.

"Three minutes to go," Kay announced.

He took Laura by the hand. "I can't believe this charm bracelet is what everybody's after," Laura exclaimed.

Jay held up the napkin he had taken from the pizza parlor and stared in disbelief. The logo on the napkin showing the pyramid-shaped slice and the Statue of Liberty with a single star shining above it was mirrored by the scene before him.

Jay had never seen a skylight like the one on this rooftop—it was a glass pyramid. The Statue of Liberty was visible over the skylight. Above Lady Liberty a single star shone in the night sky.

Snizzzz!

A crackling beam of energy streaked from the star, illuminating a large rock on the rooftop. When the glow from the star hit the rock, it revealed the rock's true nature—it was a small transporter capsule.

Crash! Roooaaar!

The glass pyramid shattered into a thousand glittering fragments as Jeff burst up through the roof, unleashing a deafening roar as he opened his huge mouth.

"Jeff! I order you to get your long self back to the subway," Jay shouted. "Or I'm gonna have to tranquilize you. And this time I'm gonna use something you won't wake up from!"

Riiiipp!

Suddenly Jeff's skin peeled away, revealing a huge, wriggling mass of neural roots. Inside the worm creature, Serleena had grown to incredible proportions.

"That's not good," said Kay.

Serleena spotted Laura and swiftly fired a neural root in her direction. Jay pushed Laura toward Kay, away from the rushing root that found Jay instead, wrapping tightly around his throat.

Serleena yanked Jay off his feet, covering his whole body with a mass of neural roots as she pulled him toward her.

"Jay!" Laura screamed.

"He'll be okay," Kay assured her, taking Laura by the arm and leading her to the transporter capsule.

Serleena, with Jay completely lost in her tangle of neural roots, leaned toward Kay and Laura. Kay blasted her with his Men in Black weaponry and sent the huge alien reeling backward.

Jay's head popped free from the tangle. "We got a hostage situation here!" he yelled. "With me being the hostage!"

Kay and Laura ran toward the transporter.

Kay turned and fired at Serleena again, but the angry Kylothian kept coming.

Jay's head burst free once again. "You're just making her mad!" he cried. "We need something with more power to stop her."

Scrad, who had followed the agents to the roof stepped forward. "How about a proton detonator?" he suggested, holding out the metallic orb Serleena had given to him.

"Yes!" Jay shouted, freeing his right arm.

Scrad tossed the detonator up to Jay, who caught it, just as he pulled himself loose from the neural roots. Jay slammed the detonator back into the mass of roots, did a back-flip, and landed on the roof right next to Scrad.

"We request asylum as political prisoners of the tyrannical Kylothians," Scrad said.

Charlie's head popped out of the backpack. "We love New York," he chimed in. "We want to stay here. It's the only place we've ever fit in."

Serleena raced toward the transporter capsule, her hideous mouth opened wide.

"Kid," began Kay, raising his weapon and aiming at Serleena. "Thanks for bringing me back."

"No problem," replied Jay, aiming his weapon as well.

Blam! Blam!

The two Men in Black weapons fired at once, blasting two small holes into the neural mass that was Serleena. She reached the transporter capsule and began to wrap her roots around it. Serleena looked down at the two holes, then back at the agents who smiled and waved good-bye.

Ka-thoom!

The proton detonator, which had lodged deep within the tangle of neural roots, exploded, destroying Serleena in a colorful burst of fireworks.

At that same moment, the transporter capsule glowed in a crackling burst of energy. When the energy burst subsided, the capsule carrying the Light was gone.

"Get their working papers in order," Kay called out to an agent. "There are always openings at the post office."

"Post office?" Scrad and Charlie shouted together,

their right hand giving their left hand a high five. "Yes!"

As a Men in Black agent led them to the van, Kay said to Jay, "Men in Black's a mess. Let's get going."

"Get going?" Jay cried as the agents all headed to their cars. "Thousands of people in New York and New Jersey must've seen the star beam! What about our famous secrecy? How are you going to explain the fact that a beam of light from above the Statue of Liberty struck a rock and turned it into a space transporter thingy?"

"Kid," Kay said, laughing and pressing a button on his digital watch. "I'll get you trained yet!"

Flash!

The torch on the Statue of Liberty lit up, sending a huge neuralyzer flash out in a fifty-mile radius. Anyone who had seen the beam of light, no longer had any memory of the event.

"I want one of those!" Jay said, as he and Kay slipped into his sedan and drove off.